THE VENGEANCE TRAIL

The stallion was still saddled, tied outside the corral. Nate mounted and was wheeling the big black around when the door opened and out rushed Winona.

"Where are you off to?"

"Zach will fill you in." ✗

Nate lit out as if rabid wolves nipped at his heels. He had to cover a lot of ground quickly. Rather than waste precious time going to where Lou and his son had been attacked by the men, he angled to the north to cut their trail. Zach had said the pair rode westward. Assuming they were headed for the same general vicinity as the night before, they had to cross a broad meadow a mile from the cabin. That was where he would pick up their trail.

In short order Nate was there, searching along the meadow's west fringe. Freshly churned earth bore out his guesswork. The imprint of shod hoofs was plain as day.

"You're mine, you mangy bastards," Nate declared as he brought the stallion to a trot. The two men had been riding at a brisk walk. Apparently, they were convinced they had given Zach and Lou the slip and assumed they were safe.

They were about to learn differently.

WILDERNESS

#26:
BLOOD FEUD

$\longleftrightarrow$

David Thompson

LEISURE BOOKS   **B**   NEW YORK CITY

To Judy, Joshua, and Shane.

A LEISURE BOOK®

January 1999

Published by

Dorchester Publishing Co., Inc.
276 Fifth Avenue
New York, NY 10001

ISBN 0-8439-4477-3

BLOOD
FEUD

Chapter One

A serpent was loose in the Garden of Eden.

Simon Ward discovered it quite by accident. A mare had broken her tether and wandered from his homestead. So for most of that sun-drenched morning he had tracked the contrary animal, finally coming on her in a glade. She was grazing, unaware of his presence.

Dismounting, Simon cat-footed through the pines. This made the third time in as many months he had to fetch the mare back. She was becoming more of a bother than she was worth. Maybe, at the next rendezvous, he would offer her for sale or trade. Let someone else have the headaches.

Simon was clad in a worn shirt and patched pants bought in Boston over a year and a half before. In his left hand was his trusty rifle. His waist was adorned with two flintlock pistols and a butcher knife. He would have liked to add a tomahawk to his arsenal, as his mentor had done, but he had not yet had occasion to obtain one. Maybe he could do that, too, at the next rendezvous.

The annual gathering of trappers had to be experienced to be believed. Simon was not a trapper and had no desire to be, but anyone could go to the rendezvous. Hundreds of Indians from various tribes attended. So did missionaries, traders, and the few settlers who called the majestic Rocky Mountains home.

Simon was one of the latter. Not all that long ago he had been a clerk at a mercantile in Boston, Massachusetts. Inspired by tales of the wonderful adventures awaiting those hardy enough to brave the wilderness, Simon had headed west with his new bride. That they lived long enough to reach the Rockies was due more to Providence than any skill on his part. That they were still alive was largely due to the mountain man who had taken Simon under his wing and taught him the skills needed to stay alive.

One of those skills involved being able to move through the woods as quietly as a great cat. Simon was not an expert at it by any means, but he was silent enough to stalk within eight feet of the mare before she detected him. For that, the wind was to blame, for it shifted at an inopportune moment and bore his scent right to her.

Snorting, the mare glanced around, spied him, and tried to bolt. As she lunged into motion, so did Simon. Taking three bounds, he hurled himself at the lead rope, which hung from her neck and trailed a good half-dozen feet behind her. His clawed right hand wrapped tight, but not before the rope had given a sharp jerk and torn skin from his palm.

Letting go of the rifle, Simon gripped the rope with both hands and stubbornly clung on. He had to dig in his heels to keep from being upended. "Whoa, there, you infernal dolt!" he hollered. "Where in blazes do you think you're going?"

The mare, dubbed Sugar by his wife, whinnied and tried to tear free. Simon stood his ground. Calling the horse Sugar, he mused, was akin to calling a grizzly Sweet. Both had similar dispositions. He had lost count of the nasty bites and kicks Sugar inflicted. Were it up to him, he would cut her up for painter bait, but his wife was too tenderhearted to permit it. More the pity.

Simon advanced, changing his tone, speaking softly, soothingly. Sugar bobbed her head and stamped, but stood still. Seizing the halter, he wagged a finger in her sassy eye. "One more fuss, just one, and so help me, wife or no wife, you'll be in a mountain lion's belly faster than I can say Andrew Jackson.''

As if she understood, Sugar bowed her head. Some might think she was being penitent for her sins. Simon knew better. She was watching him like a hawk, waiting for him to turn his back so she could take a bite out of his backside. Smiling, he tugged on the rope, then hiked a hand to cuff her. ''Felicity isn't here to protect you now, you four-legged hussy. So be careful, or else.''

Just then Simon's gaze strayed to the nearby ground, to a patch of bare earth in which there was a clear footprint not his own. Alarmed, he bent over it. Visitors to the Garden of Eden, as he called the lush valley in which he had settled, were rare. His mentor and his mentor's wife came by once a month, as regular as clockwork. Occasionally, a white-haired old mountaineer older than Methuselah stopped for a visit. Otherwise, except for a rare trapper or trader now and then, Simon saw little of other white men. So he expected the track to be that of an Indian.

Only it wasn't.

Indians never wore boots, and this was clearly a boot print. Simon wasn't the best tracker in creation, but he knew a square heel print when he saw one. The toes pointed to the east—in the direction of his cabin. Based on how clear the impression was and on the absence of dew marks, Simon concluded the print had been made earlier that very day, maybe about the same time he started out on his search for the mare.

The thought of a strange white man lurking in the vicinity of his lovely wife goaded Simon into hurrying to his sorrel and quickly mounting. The mare in tow, he brought the sorrel to a trot.

Once, Simon would not have worried in the least. Back in Boston he had been the most trusting person alive. He had believed everyone was basically honest, basically decent.

That no one ever really wanted to harm another soul. In Boston it was easy to believe that. Boston was civilized. The rule of law held sway.

In the wilderness things were different. Here the only law was survival of the strongest, the most agile, the cleverest. Life was a constant struggle; tooth and claw and cold steel pitted men against each other and the elements. Here there were men who would as soon kill a stranger as look at him, for something so paltry as a few coins in his poke. Or less savory reasons.

Simon had learned his lesson the hard way. His beloved had been captured by slavers. If not for the timely help of his mentor, she would probably be the wife of a Comanche warrior or living in virtual slavery south of the border.

Learning the truth about human nature had shocked Simon. Two decades of culture and polite society, two decades of church and Sunday school, had given him the illusion people were much nobler than many actually were. Truth was, some men were beasts. Truth was, some women were beasts. And they *liked* being that way.

Simon could never understand people like that. His upbringing had been devoted to the Golden Rule: Always do unto others as you would have them do unto you. He was always nice because he *liked* being nice, and he wrongly assumed everyone else felt the same.

Ahead rose a hill. To catch a glimpse of his cabin, Simon rode up and over, pausing on the crest. The Garden of Eden was crescent shaped, tapering at the east and west ends. A deep stream split the valley from northwest to southeast near the middle. On the east bank, across a gravel ford, stood the cabin. From the hill, a distance of only a mile, he could see it clearly, see the smoke curling from the chimney and other horses in the large corral. Of his wife there was no sign, but that was not uncommon. Simon figured she was indoors, doing one of the hundred and one chores each of them must do daily.

Applying his heels, Simon rode into the forest and made a beeline for home. In his haste he made a mistake. He realized too late the smart thing would have been to follow the tracks. Now he had lost them, and it would be sheer luck if he spotted the intruder unless the man was right out in the open.

Simon tried to think as his mentor would think. Staying calm was foremost. He had lost count of the number of times his mentor had advised him to keep his wits about him in a crisis. "In a tight fix a body needs to think clearly, and you can't if you're flustered. Train yourself to stay calm and it will give you an edge."

Simon tried now. He took deep breaths. He tried to force his body to relax. He imagined the tension draining from him like water from a sieve. It did no good. A tiny voice at the back of his mind screamed at him to hurry, hurry, hurry. In his mind's eye he saw his darling wife being savagely assaulted. It set his heart to hammering, his blood to racing. He could no more stay calm than he could stop breathing.

Minutes crawled by as slow as snails. Simon almost yipped for joy when the sorrel burst from cover in a meadow west of the stream. On the opposite side was the cabin, peaceful and picturesque. He thought of shouting but did not want to alert the intruder in case the man was close by and had not spotted him.

Holding the rifle ready for use, Simon reached the ford. He started across, then reined up. In the soft earth where the bank had long before collapsed was another footprint, a clearer, complete print. Dread spiked through him. He raced to the other side, dismounted on the fly, and bolted for the cabin.

Shoving on the wooden latch, Simon flew inside. There were only two rooms: a living room and kitchen combined, and a nook for their bed. His wife was not at the stove, not sewing, not in her rocking chair. Darting to the nook, he confirmed she was gone.

Stark fear welled up. Simon ran back outside, around the cabin, scouring the flatland in which it was nestled and the dark forest beyond. Nothing. Not a trace of her. A glance at the corral showed all the horses were accounted for, including the one she favored. So she had not gone for a ride.

Panic threatened to steal Simon's reason. Standing still, he clenched his fists and willed himself to stay calm, to think, think, think. Should he jump back on the sorrel and search for her? No! Searching blindly would be stupid. He must find her tracks. They would tell him what he wanted to know.

Starting close to the cabin, Simon roved back and forth. Right away he discovered a problem. There were so many fresh tracks, tracks she and he had made earlier, all jumbled together, it was impossible to tell which set were her last ones. Maybe his mentor could do it, but Simon was not skilled enough.

Simon did not give up, though. He walked in overlapping circles. Since she had not taken her horse or gone to the open grassland to the east and north, he concentrated on the area adjacent to the stream. His hunch was rewarded. A solitary set of his wife's small footprints led to a spot where she often went to fill their water bucket. He found the imprint of a knee, where she had knelt to dip her hand in and take a sip. From there her tracks bore to the south.

Evidently, Felicity had paralleled the stream, strolling casually along. That encouraged him, until he came to a place where two new footprints appeared. The man he had trailed had been hiding in tall grass. Now the man was stalking her, following Felicity without her being aware.

Their tracks led toward the forest.

*   *   *

Felicity Ward was a frail slip of a woman with sandy hair and a clear complexion. Despite her size, she was a bundle of tireless energy. She worked from dawn until dusk six days a week, doing menial tasks that once would have appalled her. Housework never held much appeal. Cleaning and mending clothes and the like she had always equated with utter drudgery. If someone had told her that one day she would be a contented homebody, she would have told them they were crazy.

Yet she was.

It was hard to admit that there had been a time when she would rather buy ready-made clothes than fashion attire from scratch. That she would rather send torn garments out to be stitched than stitch them herself. Or that she would rather dine out than prepare meals. She had surely been a typical modern Bostonian.

Felicity could not say exactly when the change took place. It had not been on the long trip from Boston to the frontier, when she had spent many an hour debating whether she was the most foolish person on the face of the planet for going along with Simon's harebrained notion. It had not been during the arduous trek across the prairie, when she had seldom been able to bathe or wash her hair and their meals consisted of fresh-killed animals dripping blood. No, the change had not come about until they claimed the valley as their own and built their cabin.

There was something about having a home. Something about owning land all their own. Feelings she had never known she had—or could have—overwhelmed her. She wanted to make their haven as nice as it could be. She wanted to keep it clean and neat, to add to it, to always make it better. In short, she had become exactly like her mother.

Initially, that concerned Felicity. When she was younger she vowed she would never turn out like her mother. She thought her mother lived the most boring life imaginable, a slave to housework, a victim of perpetual boredom. "Not so, child" was her mother's response when Felicity made a comment to that effect. "I do what I do for all of us because I want the best for my husband and my children. And when you do deeds out of love, you are rewarded with a happiness so pure, you can scrub a floor and whistle while you work."

To Felicity it had been a contradiction. Scrubbing floors always put her in a funk. She would rather be out playing with her friends, having fun.

But that was then. Nowadays, when Felicity scrubbed the cabin floor, she did whistle while she worked. She liked to keep their nest spotless. She loved her husband and wanted their home to sparkle. Who would have thought it?

On this bright and cheery morning, Felicity had taken an oval basket given to her by a Shoshone woman and gone out to find roots. The same woman, Winona King, had taught her which kind were edible and which were good for making herbal remedies. She needed to restock both.

Thinking of Winona as she walked through the shadowy woodland, Felicity grinned. There was another thing. Who would have thought one day she would consider an Indian her best friend in all the world? Why, back in Boston there had not been any Indians. The first one she ever saw had been in Illinois. Later, in St. Louis, they were as common as chickens, but she had not paid them much mind. After all, they were "only" Indians, little better than animals, or so she had been led to believe by the newspapers and the government. Many people felt the only good Indian was one planted six feet under.

Felicity learned differently. She had discovered Indians were just like her own kind. They were people, not animals. Some were good by nature, some were not. To paint a whole race as vile based on the behavior of some was wrong.

Winona was largely responsible for opening her eyes. Felicity had never met a kinder, gentler person, never known anyone so considerate of others, so willing to lend a hand when needed. Felicity had grown to love Winona as dearly as her own sister, and looked forward to their get-togethers with great anticipation.

The sight of a bush with tiny, shiny leaves drew Felicity to its side. The roots were the main ingredient in a potent tincture that relieved muscle aches and cramps. She often rubbed it on Simon's shoulders and back after he spent most of an afternoon chopping wood or doing other heavy labor.

The blue dress Felicity wore was one of six still fit to wear. Winona had offered to assist her in making a buckskin dress, but Felicity would rather go on wearing the clothes she was used to until they wore out. Doing so reminded her of Boston, of her parents and her siblings. The dresses were a link to her past, a past she had loved in its way as much as she now loved her new life.

Around her waist was a wide leather belt, another of Winona's gifts. From it hung a knife. Tucked under it was a pistol, a .55-caliber smoothbore she referred to as "my cannon." Her husband insisted she take it with her everywhere in case she ran into bears or whatnot. When he first suggested she always go about armed, she had balked, thinking it silly. Then one day she had been off gathering flowers and a grizzly had risen out of the undergrowth and stared at her as if sizing her up for its next meal. Thankfully, it had wandered off without molesting her. But the incident taught her a lesson. Even husbands could be right now and then.

Felicity chuckled at her thought, set down the basket, and drew her knife. As she stooped to examine the base of the bush, a twig snapped behind her with a distinct crack. She spun, her other hand dropping to the butt of the big pistol.

Something or someone was out there. Twigs did not break on their own.

Felicity was not very worried about Indians. To the north lived the Shoshones, Winona's people, the friendliest tribe in the Rockies. To the northwest were the Crows, who could be mischievous thieves at times but who rarely harmed whites.

Far to the southwest was Ute country. While the Utes were not fond of whites, Winona's husband had once done the tribe a valuable service and as a result they let his family live unmolested on the fringes of their territory.

Winona's husband had sent word to the Utes that Simon and she were his friends, and would be friends to the Utes, as well. An Ute leader had given his consent for the Wards to stay as long as they never harmed a member of the tribe.

Felicity had seen Utes once. On a hot day the summer past Simon had rushed into the cabin saying they had visitors coming. Seven Indians. They armed themselves, and Simon stood in the doorway, waiting. Unable yet to tell one tribe from another, they had no way of knowing if their visitors were friendly or hostile.

The Kings had warned them many times about the Blackfeet, Piegans, and Bloods, who routinely slew whites but who rarely came so far south.

The Indians reined up a dozen yards out. A tall man kneed his horse closer. Felicity had marveled at how bronzed his skin was, at his long braided hair. He had touched his chest and said one word: "Ute."

Simon immediately leaned his rifle against the wall and took a cup of water to the warrior as a token of friendship. The man gulped it, smiled, then admired the tin cup. When he went to give it back, Simon motioned to let the warrior know he could keep it. The Indians left. That evening, when she went to fetch water, there on the grass by the front door was a dead buck. The warrior had shown his gratitude.

Now Felicity curled her thumb around the pistol's hammer and probed the undergrowth. No movement or sounds broke the stillness. Whatever it was, it did not want her to spot it.

She hoped it might be a deer or some other harmless creature.

Then she heard the brush rustle.

Simon Ward threw caution to the breeze and sped in among the trees. He could not run as fast as he would like, because he must stay glued to the tracks. Complicating matters, his wife had meandered back and forth as if hunting for something.

The stalker had followed her awhile, then veered to the right. Simon had a choice to make. Should he press on after his wife or shadow the stalker? He picked his wife. A quarter of a mile fell behind him. Half a mile. A hole in the ground gave him a clue what she was after. Roots.

Not calling out to her was a gamble, but a necessary one if Simon was to take her stalker by surprise. Wending in among stately pines, he stopped to look and listen. Lowering the rifle's stock, he accidentally struck a rock. Not loudly, but loud enough to carry a few dozen feet. Suddenly, to the west, leaves parted. A shaggy, bearded face peered out. Simon saw beady eyes fix on him, saw a cruel slash of a mouth curl in annoyance. He brought up the rifle, but the stalker vanished in the blink of an eye.

Simon gave chase. Twice he glimpsed a bulky form. That shaggy face glanced over a shoulder once, and an icy sensation rippled down Simon's spine. It was childish, he knew. He was after a man, nothing more, nothing less. Yet he could not shake a feeling that his quarry was more beast than human, despite the stalker's grimy homespun clothes and mud-caked boots.

The man did not appear to have a gun, which was baffling. No white man with a brain larger than a turnip would venture into the wilds without one. A dependable rifle was as essential for staying alive as a set of lungs.

Simon almost shot the fellow. The chase had lasted over five minutes, and he was growing winded when the man crested a low mound. For several seconds the burly figure was silhouetted against the green canopy. Simon snapped his rifle up, pulled the hammer back, and took a hasty bead. All it would take was a squeeze of the trigger, but Simon could not do it. He could not shoot someone in the back.

The stalker ran on, unscathed. Simon pounded to the top of the mound. "Stop, you!" was on the tip of his tongue, but he never called out. The man was gone, as if a secret cavern had yawned wide and swallowed him whole. Simon halted and listened for the telltale crash of brush but heard only the wind.

Impossible, Simon mused. Warily, he descended and prowled the pines. The tracks went to the edge of a thicket, then ended. Hunkering, he raked the interior without seeing hide nor hair of the stranger. He circled around but could not find any more prints.

Simon didn't linger. Felicity was his main concern. He jogged to where he had first spotted the intruder. His wife's tracks bore to the southeast, so he did the same. Strangely, they abruptly looped to the northeast, then traveled due north, toward the cabin. Relieved she was heading home, he slowed and contemplated what to do about the mysterious stranger.

The man had invaded Eden once; he might do so again.

Felicity spied two vague shapes flitting through the forest to the west. She opened her mouth to demand they identify themselves but changed her mind. Maybe they had no idea she was there. Why advertise it and risk being taken captive, or slain?

When the crackling faded in the distance, she worked her way to the northeast to swing wide of anyone who might be dogging her footsteps. Only when she was convinced it was safe did she bear to the north and hurry homeward.

Felicity debated whether to tell her husband. Simon meant well, but he had a habit of overreacting when he thought she was in peril. He became as protective as her mother, and that was the last thing she wanted.

Felicity's mother had dominated her life from the day she learned to toddle on two legs until she finally stood on her own two feet and announced she would wed Simon whether her mother liked it or not. Her mother had ranted for weeks about how Felicity would regret it, how Simon was unfit matrimony material, how he would never amount to much.

Felicity's father had said little, as always. His opinions were never rated worthwhile by his wife, so he no longer expressed any. He sat in his chair, puffing on his pipe, mumbling "Yes, dear," whenever Felicity's mother addressed him. It always galled Felicity, how weak her father had become.

Her mother had that effect on a lot of people. Maribel Morganstern cowed them, bossed them, treated everyone as if they were inferior. Even Felicity. Until there came the day when Felicity decided enough was enough. She would not let her mother rule her life anymore. She would live as she saw fit.

Frequently, Felicity wondered if she had dated Simon because she truly liked him or to spite her mother. Truth was, Simon had not appealed to her very much at first. When she got to know him better, when she saw how sweet he was deep down, how he was always a gentleman, how he cared so deeply for her, love blossomed.

Their wedding had been the grandest day ever. Felicity had worn a special dress that had belonged to her grandmother. More than a hundred people attended, and after the vows were exchanged, everyone danced and drank and ate until after midnight. Incredibly, even her mother seemed to have a good time.

But any goodwill harvested that day was soon destroyed by Simon's decision to head west. Her relatives and his both tried to talk them out of it. Her mother threatened to disown her. His father said the same. Yet, when it became clear Simon would not relent, both families helped defray expenses and sincerely wished them well.

Suddenly the sound of something crashing through the underbrush brought Felicity up short. She whirled, extending the pistol. Whatever it was, it was almost on top of her. "Halt or I'll shoot!" she hollered, thinking if it was an animal her voice might scare it off and if it was a person they would have the common sense to stop even if they could not comprehend English.

But the thing kept on coming.

Much to Felicity's dismay, her hand started to shake. Inadvertently, her finger tightened on the trigger just as someone broke into the open.

It was Simon!

The pistol discharged with a thunderous boom.

Chapter Two

The bull elk sensed something was amiss. A splendid specimen, it raised its head and sniffed the air, testing for danger. But the wind was blowing the wrong way, and the man who had crept to within forty yards of the clearing went unnoticed. After a while the elk resumed grazing.

Nate King did not try to shoot it yet. With the patience of a born hunter, he waited for the elk to be completely at ease. Then, slowly sliding his rifle along the top of the log he was hidden behind, he aimed carefully, pulled back the hammer, and pressed his cheek to the stock. The elk raised its head again, chewing contentedly, blissfully unaware its minutes of life were numbered.

Nate held his breath to steady his aim, centered the sights on the elk's side, and smoothly stroked the trigger. Lead and smoke spewed from the muzzle. The recoil was negligible. To a man of his size, the kick of a Hawken was like the slap of a baby. The elk staggered but did not fall. Nate rose onto his knees, drawing one of the matched pair of flintlocks adorning his waist. Forty yards was a long shot for a pistol, but he had dropped targets at that range before.

There was no need. The elk tottered, spouting scarlet from nostrils and mouth. A few halting strides was all it could take. Dropping to the ground, it snorted, spattering its chest with blood. Long legs thrashed wildly as it sank onto its side.

Nate cautiously approached. Wounded elk had been known to attack those who shot them, to flail with iron hoofs or slash with rapier antlers. But his caution proved as un-necessary as a second shot. The bull was dead.

Idly aiming at a stump, Nate fired a shot anyway. It was the signal that would bring his son and his son's companion at a gallop. All three of them were eager to get home before sunset—Nate more so, since he was worried about a series of strange events that had taken place over the past week.

It had started with a feeling, a troubling sensation of being watched. On more than one occasion Nate had felt as if un-seen eyes were upon him. He would be skinning a hide or repairing a saddle and suddenly the short hairs at the nape of his neck would prickle. Several days before, on his way to the lake to fill a bucket, the sensation had been so strong that he conducted an extensive search of the surrounding woods, without result.

Then, two days later, a horse had gone missing. For a horse to stray was not unusual. For one to wander from the corral when the gate was shut most definitely was.

That very morning another incident had taken place. Nate, Zach, and Louisa had ridden out before first light, heading to the northwest. About ten miles from home, on a ridge that afforded a sweeping vista of Longs Peak and the snow-crowned summits that flanked it, Nate had stumbled on foot-prints. Puzzling footprints. A white man had made them, a big white man, someone bigger than Nate himself, and Nate was well over six feet tall. The man had been alone, on foot, trekking from north to south.

Who had it been? What was he doing there? Where was he headed? These were questions that burned in Nate all day. They required answers. Ten miles from his cabin sounded like a lot, but to Nate it was the same as if the stranger had passed with ten yards of his doorstep.

Travelers were always welcome at Nate's cabin as long as they were friendly. Those who weren't soon learned why Nate had a reputation among the trapping fraternity as being one coon it was wise to avoid when he was riled. Maybe it had something to do with the name bestowed on him by a Cheyenne: Grizzly Killer. Or maybe it was because anyone who tried to harm him always wound up worm food.

Nate was anxious to take up the trail of the giant and find out where the man had gone. First things first, though. Sliding the ramrod from its housing under the barrel of his Hawken, he reloaded the rifle and the pistol. As he finished, hooves drummed. Two riders came toward him, side by side.

On the right was Nate's oldest, Zachary King. Not quite eighteen, the boy looked more Indian than white. His buckskins, his moccasins, his hair were all worn Shoshone-style. "You beat me to it, Pa," he declared, smiling. "I should have known you'd win."

Nate smiled. His son referred to a bet they had made as to who would bring down an elk first. "I don't see what you wanted twenty dollars for, anyhow. That's a heap of money."

Zach glanced at Louisa. He was embarrassed to say it, but he wanted it for her. For a very special gift. Sighing, he responded, "Oh, well. Having to tote water, chop wood, and tend the horses for a week all by myself won't kill me."

The significance of the glance was not lost on Nate. His son and the young woman had taken a powerful shine to each other. "Cow eyes," his friend Shakespeare McNair called the looks they swapped. "Climb down and we'll get to work. Ever skinned an elk before, Louisa?"

Louisa May Clark nodded. Wiry and lean, she wore baggy buckskins and cropped her hair short. From a distance she could easily pass for a boy. By design. To spare her from rude advances, her father had thought up the ruse. And it worked. In every frontier settlement they passed through on their journey west, not one male had caught on. "Yes, sir, Mr. King. Don't you remember? I helped Stalking Coyote cut up one when we first met."

"I remember," Nate said. Stalking Coyote was his son's Shoshone name. For some reason Louisa preferred it over Zach's Christian one. "Let's get cracking, then."

Louisa slid off and set right to work. She did not mind the blood and the gore. Nor did she become queasy at the sight of coiled intestines and other internal organs. During the many months spent trapping with her father, she had skinned three or four animals a day, whether beaver for plews or game for the supper pot.

Zach squatted beside her, admiring her skill. She was unlike any white girl he had ever met. True, he had not met many, except for the time his parents took him to St. Louis. But he had been much younger then.

It was only recently that Zach had begun to notice the opposite sex. He observed quirky things at the outset, such as how they walked and how they smelled and how their bosoms jiggled when they ran. His father told him it was normal, that all males went through the same change. He had refused to believe it was happening to him. He'd had no interest in women and would never have an interest, not if he could help it. Which was exactly his father's point. He couldn't help it. No male could. Nature always took its course regardless of human wishes.

So Zach reached the point where he noticed everything about females. Particularly about Louisa. How her hair curled around her ears. How her jaw muscles twitched when she worked. How supple she was, how graceful. How her eyes glowed when she gazed at him.

That Zach cared for her so much surprised no one more than him. She was not a beauty by most standards. She did not have the rich black hair or full body of a Shoshone. Nor did she possess the creamy softness or saucy bearing of a white. Louisa was unique, a combination of traits he had never beheld in any other. Perhaps that was why he liked her so much. Why sometimes his heart ached with longing. Why, at night, he would take her on long walks and kiss her until his lips felt fit to burn off.

"Hey, you almost cut me, silly goose."

Zach blinked, and straightened. He had slashed into the elk close to Lou's fingers. "Sorry."

Nate King turned, pretending to be interested in a raven soaring overhead so they would not see his smirk. By the age of ten, Zach could carve up a carcass as expertly as men twice his age. Of late, though, the boy had become remarkably absentminded. "I'd best fetch the rest of the horses," Nate mentioned. Walking briskly off, he noted that the sun was on its downward arc. Making it home by nightfall was unlikely, but he would do the best he could.

Memories of his own youth washed over the mountain man. Recollections of when he met Winona, of how they fell for one another at first sight. There was no predicting love. The human heart pulsed to rhythms often beyond the control of the heart's owner. But he had no regrets. Taking Winona for his wife had been the smartest thing he ever did. She was his joy, his treasure, his life. And if his son felt the same about Louisa May Clark, neither heaven nor hell could stem the tide of their devotion.

The three packhorses and Nate's stallion were in a gully a quarter of a mile to the northeast. Nate had left them there when he spotted the elk and gone on afoot. It had taken him the better part of an hour to get close enough for a perfect shot. For him that was important. While feeding his family and earning a livelihood demanded Nate slay game, he did not like the animals to suffer. He always tried to bring them down with a single, well-placed shot to the brainpan or the heart.

Some mountaineers were not quite as conscientious. They fired even when they did not have clear shots. They inflicted painful wounds, then had to track the stricken creatures for miles to put them out of their misery. More often than not, the hunters gave up and went after something else.

With his own eyes, Nate once saw a man put twenty-two lead balls into a buffalo. Enough to wipe out a small herd. Yet the man's marksmanship was so poor, the riddled bull did not go down. Nate had to dispatch it because the other man ran out of ammo.

The horses were right where Nate had left them. Nate rejoined his son and the young woman, and helped carve up the elk. The hide was saved and would be cured when they got home. The meat, the hooves, even the skull was strapped onto a packhorse. Only the guts and a few scraps were left; they would be devoured by scavengers.

Nate took much more than most white men would. Living with the Shoshones had taught him never to let any part of a kill go to waste. The skull, for instance, would be cracked open and the brain extracted. It would be dissolved in warm water, then simmered into a thin paste, which was rubbed on the hair side of the hide to treat it. Bones were used to make awls and scrapers. Hoofs were a main ingredient in glue.

Even more uses were found for buffalo. Nate had totaled them up once and was astounded to discover his adopted people relied on the shaggy brutes for eighty-eight everyday items, things like blankets and robes, lodge covers and parfleches. Bowstrings were made from bull sinew, arrowheads from buffalo bone, shields from the thick hide around a bull's neck, knives from the hide on its sides.

Boats, snowshoes, travois hitches, lariats, hackamores, the Indians owed them all to the buffalo. Tobacco pouches were made from calf hide. Berry pouches were fashioned from the hides of unborn calves, because they resisted staining and leakage. So highly prized were buffalo calves that after a hunt Indian women were quick to cut the calves out of all the pregnant cows.

Cooking vessels were made from buffalo paunches. Water buckets too. Horns made excellent spoons and cups. Hairbrushes were made from the rough side of the tongue. Tails were used to make swatters for killing flies. Soap came from buffalo fat. Not even the buffalo's dung went to waste; it was fuel for fires.

Many tribes were totally dependent on the great beasts. Should the buffalo ever die out, Nate did not know what they would do. But that was highly unlikely. Buffalo numbered in the millions, in herds so vast it took a whole week for the teeming rivers of muscle and hair to pass by.

Indians believed the buffalo would exist for as long as there were stars in the sky. Nate tended to agree. Then he would think of the beaver, and how trapping had so reduced their number that they were on the verge of being wiped out. What would happen if one day settlers poured onto the prairie and thronged the mountains? Would the buffalo be killed off? The notion was not as far-fetched as it sounded. Once only thirteen colonies existed. Now cities and towns teemed between the Atlantic Ocean and the Mississippi River, with more springing up every year.

Nate would hate to see the wilderness overrun. It was the last refuge for those who yearned to live free, for those who refused to be slaves to law and custom, who would rather die than have self-righteous politicians tell them how they should live. Nate could never go back. Once having tasted life as the Almighty meant it to be, no man in his right mind would give it up to live in a cage.

Zachary King had something else on his mind. It was the same dilemma he'd been pondering for weeks now, ever since he met Louisa May Clark.

Zach wanted her to be his mate, his wife. But he was at a loss as to how to go about broaching the subject to her. Especially since Lou had once commented that she had no interest in marriage whatsoever.

As for his folks, the one time he'd mentioned it, they'd

looked at him as if he'd been stomped in the head by a buffalo. He fretted they would object, they'd say he was too young, that he should wait. Yet he knew many Shoshones his age who had wives, and he was just as mature as they were.

It shocked him, though, wanting to marry a white girl. Until recently he had not thought highly of his father's people. All the hatred and abuse he had suffered were to blame.

In the white man's eyes Zach was a "half-breed," an object of contempt and scorn. An accident of birth had branded him a 'breed for life. He had just about decided he wanted nothing more to do with whites, that except for his father and Uncle Shakespeare and a few of his father's friends, he would shun the white man as they shunned him.

Then along came Lou.

While growing up, Zach had always admired how deeply in love his folks were. He saw it in their eyes, in the things they did for each other. Often, he had pondered the secret of love: What was it? Would he know it when he felt it? Would he ever feel it, or was he destined to go through life alone? Love had been one of the monumental mysteries of life.

It was a mystery no more. Zach loved Lou with every fiber of his being. He could not stop staring at her when they were together and not stop thinking of her when they were apart. Before they met, his daydreams were of glory in battle, of coups counted, of earning honors due mighty warriors. Now he daydreamed about her during the day and dreamed about her at night. She was his whole world, his whole universe. The thought of going through life without her caused a cold hand to clutch his heart.

What should he do about it? Should he propose? Many an evening over the years, while seated snug and warm in front of the fireplace, Zach had listened to his parents relate how they had first met, the events that resulted in their being husband and wife. His father had never gotten down on bended knee to formally propose, as was traditional with white men. But should Zach do that? Should he ask Lou to marry him as a white man would?

So many questions, so few answers.

At that moment, Louisa May Clark was asking a question of her own: How much longer would she stay with the Kings? She did not want to impose, yet neither could she bear to leave Stalking Coyote. He had become everything to her. He was her joy, her life. He put a smile on her lips the first thing each morning and scorched those same lips with hot kisses the last thing each night.

Lord, how she wanted him! Her feelings bewildered her at times. They were so strong, so potent. Her dear departed mother had told her that one day she would undergo a "change," that she would view men in a whole new light. But Lou never imagined anything like this. She never imagined caring for a man so much that she could not bear the thought of living without him.

Part of her confusion over what to do stemmed from the fact that Stalking Coyote had not told her he loved her. His fondness for her went without saying. Their nightly walks confirmed as much. But she needed to know how deep that fondness ran. Was it pure physical passion, or did he love her as she loved him? And if he did, why hadn't he said so? Should she bring it up? Should she take the bit in her mouth and come right out with how she felt?

Lou wished her folks were alive to advise her. Her mother, Mary Bonham Clark, had been the sweetest woman who ever lived. Her father, Zebulon Clark, had been a fine father and done his best to rear Lou alone after Mary passed on. Lou could not bear to think of his last moments, when hostile Indians swept out of nowhere and laid him low with an arrow in his ribs. That she was still alive was a miracle. That she loved Zach King was another.

What to do? What to do?

Lou just didn't know.

Nate King pushed hard to reach his homestead before the sun set, but they were still five miles away when the blazing orb dipped below castlelike ramparts to the west. Sunsets in the Rockies were usually spectacular, and this one was no exception. The invisible hand of the Almighty painted the horizon with vivid hues of red, orange, and pink.

As Nate started to turn his head, movement caught his eye. On a ridge to the southwest were two horsemen. They were too far away for him to note details. He kept on riding so they wouldn't suspect he had seen them, and when he was in among pines, he drew rein and shoved the lead rope at his son. "Take this. Tell your mother I spotted a couple of strange coons. I'm going to see who they are."

Zach was stunned. He should have seen them too, but he had been absorbed in thought about Louisa.

"Stick to heavy cover and keep your eyes skinned," Nate said. Smacking his heels against the stallion, he angled to the right.

"Let me go with you."

"No. Where there are two there might be more. Stay at the cabin with the ladies and your sister."

Zach understood. If the worst came to pass, if hostiles were abroad, his father was relying on him to help safeguard the women and their home. "Don't you worry, Pa. We can take care of ourselves."

Lou could not say what sparked her to pipe up with "How about me, Mr. King? I'd be glad to tag along."

Nate admired her spunk, but he declined. To lessen the sting he said, "I know you're a good shot. Zach will want you at his elbow if the Blackfoot Confederacy is paying us a visit. The last time we went up against them, we were lucky to keep our hair."

The mountain man trotted down the slope. Following his own advice, he never exposed himself to the pair on the ridge. He saw them from time to time, though, off through the trees. He regretted not packing his spyglass in the two beaded parfleches that served as his saddlebags. If he had, he could tell if the riders were white or red, and if red, which tribe they were from.

The ridge was only half a mile distant, but reaching it took over half an hour. Nate chose a roundabout route so he came up on the duo from the rear. A steep slope littered with talus had to be negotiated, Nate picking his route with care to avoid giving himself away. A stone's throw from the rim, Nate stopped and climbed down. He wrapped the reins around a rock, then stalked higher. His moccasin-shod feet made no more noise than would a mouse. At the summit he crouched low.

No sounds indicated the pair were still there. Nate uncoiled, leveling the Hawken at the spot where they had been. Sure enough, they were gone. Frowning, he strode over to inspect the ground. Hoofprints were all he found. One of the horses had been shod, one had not. The two men—if they were both men—had headed due south. He estimated they had a five-minute head start.

Hastening to the stallion, Nate forked leather and galloped in pursuit. A tract of dense forest gave way to a tableland dotted with boulders the size of his cabin. Washes and ravines had to be crossed or skirted. The ground was hard-packed, so the tracks were faint and growing fainter, thanks to the gathering twilight.

Soon it was almost too dark to see. Nate forged on, though. He had to be sure the pair had not turned toward his cabin. For all he knew, these two might be the ones who had been spying on him. He would like to learn why.

With the advent of night, the woods came alive with new sounds. Nighttime was predator time, when the beasts that fed on other beasts came out of their dens and caves to feast until the sun rose.

The wavering, lonesome howl of a wolf was the cue for other predators to let the world know they were on the prowl. Painters screeched like tormented women. Grizzlies grunted and rumbled in monstrous disdain. Coyotes yipped in feral chorus.

Assorted screams and outcries punctuated the bedlam.

The stallion was not fond of being abroad after dark. It moved with inbred caution, ears pricked, nostrils constantly flaring to catch wind-borne scents.

The likelihood of encountering a meat-eater did not bother Nate. Wolves avoided humans unless starved. Coyotes posed no threat whatsoever. Painters—or cougars, as some had taken to calling them—normally attacked only when provoked. Grizzlies were the greatest danger. As unpredictable as they were temperamental, they were the kings of their domain. For sheer ferocity no living creature matched them.

The last of the light faded.

Nate rode on, expecting to spot the campfire of those he sought. Myriad stars lent the landscape an eerie pale glow. He avoided a deep, narrow ravine, roving along the rim until he found a spot where the two sides had buckled to form an earthen ramp. The stallion floundered in soft dirt on the way down but stayed upright.

The farther Nate traveled, the more perplexed he grew. Riding at night was risky. Most would stop and make camp. But the two he was after apparently had no such inclination. For as far as the eye could see, an inky mantle cloaked the wilds.

Going on was pointless, but Nate did so anyway. He figured the pair had somehow realized he was on their heels and had gone to ground. He might have passed them already. That they were lying low tended to confirm his suspicions.

Men who had nothing to hide would not take to cover. Men who were up to no good would.

By Nate's reckoning it was nine o'clock when he chose to head home. Further searching was pointless. Mountains towered like Titans on all sides. Rounding the base of one, he twisted to open a parfleche. Winona had packed enough jerky and pemmican to feed an army. He selected a piece of each and was raising the jerky to his mouth when a shot rang out.

A leaden hornet buzzed past Nate's ear. Dropping the food, he hauled on the reins. A wispy cloud of smoke pinpointed the location of the shooter, sixty yards above. The would-be killer had to have the eyesight of a painter to make a shot like that.

Nate spurred the stallion into a headlong charge, the last thing the ambusher would expect. There was a method to his madness. By charging, he would not give the man time to reload. Stones clattered out from under the stallion's flying hoofs as he rapidly narrowed the gap. A shifting patch of blackness alerted him the shooter was on the move, fleeing to the west. Nate jammed the Hawken against his shoulder and fired.

The rider cried out but did not slacken speed. Within moments he had raced into a large stand of aspen.

Palming a pistol, Nate plowed in among the slender boles. When he came out the other side the slope was empty. Reining up, he glanced right and left. His quarry had given him the slip.

Fuming at being duped, Nate plunged back into the stand. He searched it from end to end. When that failed to turn up the culprit, he roamed the slope above, then the slope below. Whoever it was had gone, melting into the night like a will-o'-the-wisp.

Bafflement and fury boiled in Nate like water in a hot spring. Now there could be no doubt the pair had evil intent.

They had tried to slay him once, and they would try again. Neither he nor his family were safe until they were caught. He had half a mind to make a cold camp and resume the hunt in the morning, but he could not bring himself to leave Winona and the others alone that long. Anxiety for his loved ones ate at him like acid.

Reluctantly, Nate rode eastward. He made a mental note to get word to his two nearest neighbors, Shakespeare McNair and Simon Ward. They must be warned. Here they were, hundred of miles from civilization, living in remote valleys far up in mile-high mountains, and they had to be on their guard against common cutthroats!

What was the world coming to?

Chapter Three

Hours earlier, Simon Ward stared into the muzzle of imminent death and opened his mouth to shout, to tell his wife there was no need to shoot. It was only him. But he did not yell soon enough. For at that instant her pistol discharged. With only fifteen feet separating them, evading the slug was out of the question. Simon was a dead man. Or he would have been, had Felicity's hand not been shaking. The ball whizzed within a whisker's width of Simon's left ear, then thudded into a tree trunk.

"Simon!" Felicity exclaimed, horrified at what she had nearly done. Rushing up, she threw her arms around him. "Oh, Simon! I didn't know it was you. I thought someone was stalking me."

Simon felt weak at the knees. He'd had close shaves, but never one that close. Clearing his throat, he said, "There was someone. I saw him. A bearded guy. He ran off, and I couldn't catch him." Holding her close enough to feel her heart pound, he tenderly kissed her neck. "I was worried something had happened to you. I couldn't bear it if anything did." Without her, he would not want to go on living.

Felicity pulled back to scan the forest. "Was it a trapper, do you think? Why didn't he show himself? What was he afraid of?"

Simon shrugged. "Who can say?" In order not to upset her, he did not let on how anxious he was for her safety. An ordinary trapper would not have done what the bearded man

35

did. Taking her hand, he started homeward. "We'll both stick close to the cabin today in case the stranger comes back."

His eyes gave him away. Felicity often joked that Simon wore his feelings on his sleeve, when in truth he wore them in his eyes. She saw he was worried, and she grew worried. The memory of her ordeal with the slavers was all too fresh. She suffered regular nightmares. Afterward, she would wake up in a cold sweat, gasping for air, terrified she was back in their clutches. Her friend, Winona, said it took a long time to get over so horrible an experience. Felicity was beginning to wonder if she ever would.

The cabin stood bathed in sunlight. Butterflies flitted above the flowers Felicity had planted. By the stream a doe drank. The sorrel and Sugar were nipping at grass.

Simon was glad all was well. Maybe he was fretting for no reason. Maybe it had been a trapper, after all. One of those odd recluses who lived like hermits, hardly ever having contact with other people.

"I'll get supper started, darling."

Simon unsaddled the sorrel and put both horses in the corral. Sugar tried to take a bite out of his arm, so he swatted her on the nose none too gently. After surveying the valley, he shouldered the saddle and joined his wife.

The rest of the day was uneventful. Simon cleaned his guns, then sorted through seeds he had special ordered from St. Louis. A trader had picked them up for him and brought them to the last rendezvous. Corn, wheat, barley, tomatoes, potatoes, lettuce, and others. Enough to start his own farm.

Some of the trappers had poked fun at him for going to all that trouble for a bunch of seeds. They had laughed at him for thinking he could grow crops in the mountains. No one had ever done it, they said. But that did not mean no one ever could.

The seeds were the key to Simon's future, to the family

Felicity and he planned to raise. He believed crops would thrive in the fertile upland valleys, despite the shorter growing season. All it would take was the right seeds, the right plants. Then he could supply all the food his family would ever need, plus have extra to trade for the few essentials they could not provide on their own.

Which was precious little. They had no rent to pay, no mortgage on their homestead. All the water they'd ever need was right outside their door. Between the abundant wildlife and the crops he'd raise, food would never be a problem. Their store-bought apparel would eventually wear out, but when it did, they would make new garments rather than buy more. His mentor had taught him how to cure buckskin so wonderfully soft, it rivaled the best tailor-made clothing.

That left tools and the like. Most of the implements he needed he had already acquired, thanks to funds saved prior to the journey west. When new tools were needed, he would barter for them. The traders who plied their wares at the rendezvous brought in everything under the sun.

Only thing was, rumor had it the days of the rendezvous would soon end. There were so few beaver, it was not worth the effort for merchants to make the long trek across the plains. But Simon wasn't overly troubled by the reports. Mountain men were forever journeying to St. Louis on some pretext or another. He could always impose on them to obtain whatever he needed. Or he could trade with the pilgrims bound for the Oregon country.

Simon liked being self-sufficient. In Boston he had been dependent on others for everything. For the money he earned, the food he ate, the clothes he wore. Even for the roof over his head. He had been a slave to society, weaned in a culture where everyone was so accustomed to having things done for them, no one knew how to do anything for themselves anymore.

Here in Eden, Simon was his own man. Here, he and Felicity met their own needs by the sweat of their brow. In the wilderness a person had to learn to stand on his or her own feet or they were crushed under the grinding heel of their own incompetence. The threat of starvation was always only a few meals away. The elements lurked like medieval monsters, ready to freeze the unprepared with an icy blast of wintry breath or to fry the foolish in a scorching blaze of summer heat.

A man had to be self-sufficient or he died. It was as simple as that.

Felicity busied herself at the counter and stove. She'd made a fresh loaf of bread early that morning. For their meal, she would serve venison steak, squirrel soup, and boiled roots. Dessert was a pudding Winona had shown her how to prepare. Simon could wash everything down with plenty of rich black coffee. She'd savor some tea. It was, in short, a feast for royalty.

Felicity thought of her cousin, Ethel, and wondered what Ethel was doing at that very moment. Shopping for the latest fashions? Dining at a fancy restaurant? Getting ready to go to a play or attend a concert?

There were days when Felicity missed the frills civilization offered. She would love to be able to go to the theater now and then. To hear an orchestra. To listen to a poetry recital. To stroll along a downtown avenue admiring the dresses on display in the shops. Ah, those were the days!

Catching herself, Felicity grinned. Old pleasures were as hard to give up as old habits. The simpler life she now led appealed to her just as much as life in Boston ever had. Certainly, she missed her relatives and friends, but not enough to persuade Simon to leave their haven.

She could, if she wanted. He would do anything for her. A few tears rendered him clay in her hands, to be molded as she saw fit. But she would not do that to him. Eden was his dream. Their dream. She had gone into this with an open mind and open heart. It would not be proper for her to back out now, after they had gone through so much hardship.

Still, Felicity could not help but think how much safer they would be back in Boston. No wild beasts to contend with, no bloodthirsty Blackfeet or bearded strangers to be on the lookout for.

"I think I'll write my cousin and ask her to come visit."

Simon looked up from the wooden box that held their future. "Ethel? She won't step foot outside Boston. Her idea of roughing it is to go a full day without washing her hair."

"She's prissy, I agree, but she's not that bad. When we were little we camped outside a few times."

"In her backyard, as I recall. So she could run inside when she was hungry or thirsty or had to use a chamber pot. And squeal for her mommy if a mosquito buzzed by."

"Ethel can't help being how she is. She was raised in the city."

"City life is slavery. We get so used to being waited on hand and foot that we don't realize the price we've paid. The freedoms our forefathers fought for are being whittled away by our own laziness."

Felicity knew she should not have gotten him started. He could go on for hours about the seductive evils of society. "I still think Ethel might come. As a lark if for no other reason. So she can go back and tell everyone how simply primitive we've become."

"If that's the case, we shouldn't disappoint her. I'll go around in a loincloth and you can make a buckskin dress and wear feathers in your hair. We'll eat our meat raw and scratch at ourselves as if we have lice. And we won't take baths for a month before she arrives."

"Simon Ward! We'll do no such thing. That would be downright mean."

"And downright hilarious. I'd love to see how long she

can hold her breath. Or maybe she'll just pinch her nose shut the whole time she's here.''

Felicity could not contain her mirth. ''You're awful sometimes. You know that? Positively horrendous.''

''I try, my dear. I try.''

The next morning dawned crisp and clear. Felicity was up first, as usual. She nudged Simon, but he mumbled something about her wearing him out and rolled back over. Grinning, she slid into her robe, donned her slippers, and padded to the counter. It was part of their daily ritual for her to put on a pot of coffee and fill the cabin with its fragrance before Simon would rouse himself.

As Felicity poured water from the bucket into the pot she heard a series of low clomps outside, as if a horse were stamping its hoof. Then one nickered. ''Did you hear that?''

''What?''

''Sounds like the horses are acting up.''

''It's probably those stupid coyotes again. Ever since I cut up that buck and forgot to bury what was left, they keep coming around. If they don't stop, you'll have a coyote rug before long.''

Again the horse nickered, louder than before. Simon sat up, blinking to clear his eyes and his head. ''That's my sorrel.''

''How can you tell?''

''I just can.''

Nate had instructed Simon to get to know each of their horses as well as he knew himself. To learn how they differed, to memorize their hoofprints so he could tell one from the other. To do the same with the sounds they made. For just as no two people sounded alike, no two horses whinnied the same. Simon had thought it silly to go to so much effort, but his mentor assured him one day the knowledge would come in handy.

Throwing off the quilt, Simon rose and pulled on his pants and boots. Thinking he only had to shoo coyotes away, he left his shirt draped over the bedpost and walked to the door. His rifle and two spares were on a rack beside it. "I'll only be a minute."

In the glorious rosy glow of a new day the Garden of Eden was spectacular. White fluffy clouds sailed on lofty currents. The stream was a turquoise blue, gurgling like a happy baby. To the south deer quenched their thirst, among them a fragile fawn. Dew glistened on the grass like shimmering diamonds.

Goose bumps broke out on Simon as he headed around the cabin. He was not quite fully awake, and he was in an irritable frame of mind. Being lured outdoors before jolting his system with coffee was not to his liking. He went around the corner, declaring, "All right, you miserable coyotes. This is the last straw. Scamper elsewhere or suffer the consequences."

"Well, ain't you-all the feisty one."

Simon nearly tripped over his own feet in consternation. Next to the corral was a young woman about his own age. She had long, greasy black hair. A plain homespun dress, frayed at the hem, clung loosely to her slender frame. Her cheeks, her arms, her lower legs were smudged with dirt, and incredibly, she was barefoot, her feet positively filthy. "What in the world?" he blurted.

"And a fine howdy-do to you, too, mister," said the apparition. She had a twang to her voice, a heavy southern accent.

"Where did you come from, girl?"

She grinned, revealing that one of her upper front teeth was missing. "I ain't no girl, mister. I'm a full-growed woman. I've done my share of sparkin', I'll have you know."

"Sparkin'?" Simon was desperately trying to get his befuddled brain to work, but it refused.

Her grin widened. "You know, courtin' and such. Don't tell me a handsome feller like you ain't never sparked? That's hardly likely, seein' as how you've got a woman. She your wife, handsome?"

Simon was too flabbergasted to answer. So someone else did.

"That's enough out of you, Cindy Lou. Watch that trollop tongue of yours or you'll fetch a switchin'. Woman or no, you're never too old for me to beat the livin' tar out of you. Learn proper manners, hussy, or else."

Simon pivoted, his amazement growing. A heavyset man every bit as grungy as Cindy Lou sat astride a mule that appeared to be all bone and gristle. He wore ragtag clothes and a floppy brown hat. Cradled in his left elbow was a Kentucky rifle. Jutting from his belt was the longest knife Simon had ever set eyes on. "Who are you? What the devil are you doing here?"

The man had small, dark eyes that glittered like embers. "Ol' Satan got nothin' to do with this, friend. I'm Jacob Coyfield. That there's my daughter. We'd be obliged if we could light and set a spell, seein' as how we've been on the go pretty near three months now."

"We're from Arkansas," Cindy Lou said.

Jacob Coyfield's flabby jowls pinched together. "When the man wants our life story, I'll give it to him. Meanwhile, why don't you learn when to speak and when to shush." He sighed. "Ever notice, mister? You can pound sense into your brood until kingdom come and there ain't no guarantee any of it will take root. Some young'uns have nothin' but rocks betwixt their ears." Coyfield rubbed the stubble on his oval chin. "So, what'll it be, friend? You going to be neighborly or not? We welcome?"

Simon had an urge to say no. Judging someone by first impressions was misleading, but he did not much like this man. Yet how could he refuse? The Christian thing to do was invite them in. And Felicity would relish having another woman to talk to. "Of course you are. Climb on down."

Jacob Coyfield winked at his daughter. "See? Be friendly to folks and they're always friendly back. Your ma and the rest will be tickled pink."

"The rest?" Simon said.

Coyfield shifted in the saddle and pumped an arm. "It's all right!" he hollered. "Bring them on in, Mabel!"

Simon was stunned to see a knot of riders emerge from the trees to the east. Five, six, seven in all, four on horses, three on mules. In the lead rode a woman every bit as plump as Jacob. She dressed like him, too, in britches and a baggy man's shirt and floppy black hat. "Who are they?"

"Kin," Coyfield said. "Our clan, or what's left of 'em after the McErnys got through. Lost my own pa about a year ago to those murderin' vermin. I'd've stayed until the last man was standin', but I had my family to think of. The feud ain't worth all their lives."

"Feud?"

"Tell me, mister. Do you make a habit of repeating everything a body says? Yes, a feud. Us hill folk have what you might call a code we live by, a code we've been livin' by since before your grandpappy was toddlin' in diapers. A code we brought with us from the Old Country. It's plain as the nose on your face that you're a Yankee, so I ain't surprised you don't know much about our ways."

"He don't know much about anything, Pa," Cindy Lou commented.

"Be civil, girl."

Simon was growing uneasy under Cindy Lou's stare. She looked at him as if he were a slab of meat she was fixing to cut up and eat. "It's true I've never been to Arkansas. The farthest south I've ever been is Maryland. Baltimore."

Jacob Coyfield had opened a pouch and inserted two pudgy fingers. "I been to New York once. Thought I'd died and gone to hell. All them people runnin' around like chickens with their heads chopped off. All that noise and confusion. I don't hardly see how anyone can abide it.''

"City life always had the same effect on me.''

"Do tell.'' Coyfield withdrew a wad of tobacco and crammed it into his mouth. Chewing noisily, he remarked, "I'd've thought all Yankees were at home in the big city. But then, what do I know? Me being a simple country boy and all.''

His sarcasm was thick enough to slice with a razor. Simon wondered if it had been directed at him personally. "Where are you headed, Jacob? If you don't mind my asking?''

Cindy Lou tittered, then blanched when her father gave her a withering glare. "We're on our way to Oregon,'' Coyfield said. "We hear tell there's good land up there for the takin'. The climate is supposed to be nice, except for a few days of rain now and again. But shucks, rain won't bother us none. Rain is the good Lord's way of washin' His creation.''

Strange words coming from a man who looked as if he had not touched soap and water in ages. Simon merely smiled and nodded. "At one time I toyed with the idea of going there. Then I heard about the Rockies.''

Jacob appraised the regal peaks ringing the valley. "It sure enough is Paradise here, ain't it? More critters than I ever saw, and plenty of water. And all these mountains stretchin' clear to heaven. Sort of puts the States to shame. I'm a mite surprised more folks haven't staked claims here.''

"They will. Give it a few years. Once word spreads, homesteads will spring up all over.''

Coyfield's relations arrived, and Jacob introduced them. In addition to his wife, Mabel, there was another woman a few years older than Cindy Lou. Her name was Mary Beth, and she was the daughter of Coyfield's brother, Samuel. Samuel had two sons, Tinder and Bo. Jacob had two sons of his own,

Jess and Cole. All four were strapping, grim men with bushy beards.

Simon studied them closely, his unease growing. One might be the stalker from the previous day, but he could not say which because he had not had a good enough look at the man's face. He was tempted to tell them he had changed his mind and they were not welcome, but that would be rude. "Why don't all of you climb down and I'll bring out the coffee." He did not deem it wise to invite them in.

"Any chance of gettin' some vittles?" Jacob asked. "I'm plumb starved."

Plump Mabel Coyfield was a cheery soul, the kind who wore a smile like a second skin. "If'n it's no bother, of course," she said. "I'd be glad to help your missus out. Me and the girls are passable cooks, if'n I say so myself. Our possum stew was the talk of the hills. And our hominy would melt in your mouth."

"Wait here. Please."

Simon was in such haste to get inside, he came close to bumping heads with Felicity, who was on her way out.

"I heard two voices and a shout. Are Nate and Winona here? I know they're due soon."

"No, it's not them." Simon sorely wished it were. "We have other company. A clan, they call themselves. Six men and three women—" Simon got no further. He was going to warn her that one of the men might be the fellow who had been spying on her, but she didn't let him finish. At the mention of women her features lit up like a lantern and she brushed past in a swirl of dress and apron. "Wait!"

Felicity darted to the corner of the cabin, overjoyed to think she would have other ladies to talk to. Her elation evaporated when she saw the whole clan. As one, they focused on her, and the tallest of the bearded men gave a start, as if he had been pricked by a needle. Felicity reminded herself that a book should never be judged by its cover. Mustering a warm smile, she advanced, holding out her hand toward the oldest woman. "I'm Felicity Ward. I can't tell you what a treat this is."

Mabel Coyfield introduced herself, adding as she inspected Felicity from head to toe, "Well, ain't you a dainty bundle of vinegar and vim. We wouldn't want to inconvenience you none. That husband of yours was lookin' right poorly."

"Pay no attention to him. He's a man."

Mabel's whole belly shook with hearty guffaws. "I can see I'm going to like you, little sister. We see eye to eye where menfolk are concerned. Odd critters, ain't they? Makes you think they was all in the outhouse when the Almighty handed out common sense."

Favorably impressed by the woman's kind bearing and humor, Felicity said, "Tell you what, Mrs. Coyfield. We have more than enough to feed your whole family—if you're hungry, that is. Care to lend a hand?"

"Land sakes, dearie. We're famished. And you plumb took the words right out of my mouth. I just told your husband we'd be happy to do what we can." Mabel glanced at the bearded man who had given a start. "Hear her, Cole? Ain't she a peach? Can't I pick 'em?"

"How's that?" Felicity asked.

Mabel gestured. "Oh, he's of the opinion Yankees never amount to much. But I told him that folks is folks no matter what part of the country they're from. You can't help being born in the wrong part, so we can't hold it against you."

"I should hope not," Felicity bantered. "Now, come. We'll talk about how terrible men are while we fix their food."

"Maybe we should add some poison," Mabel said, then playfully jabbed an elbow into Felicity's side. "A few less menfolk won't be missed, eh?"

"Well, I'd never go that far."

Simon had overheard everything. Helpless to object, he stood back as his wife and her new friends strolled inside, leaving him alone with the men. Jacob had a bulge in his left cheek the size of a walnut, dark spittle dribbling over his chin. Samuel Coyfield had leaned on a rail and was examining the cabin. He had a hawkish face etched by deep lines. His two sons and Jacob's two boys mimicked statues, as if waiting to be told what to do.

"So," Simon said to start some conversation. "What do you fellows plan to do when you get to Oregon? Farm?"

Jacob's brows puckered. "Oregon? Oh, we figure to cross that bridge when we get to it. A man has to adapt to whatever comes along."

Without being obvious, Simon scrutinized the sons, seeking to identify which one it had been. It stretched coincidence to the breaking point to believe they just happened to show up the day after the incident.

"Cole," Jacob Coyfield unexpectedly said.

"I beg your pardon?"

"You're tryin' to figure out which of these lunkheads was nosin' around your place, ain't you? It was my oldest, Cole. We had made camp yonder"—Jacob wagged a hand at the woodland—"and I sent him to rustle up some grub. He seen your missus and followed her a spell. Not to hurt her, you understand. He's always been shy, and he was afeared to show himself. Then you showed up."

"Why did he run away like that?"

"He reckoned you might shoot him. Back where we come from, lookin' at another man's woman can get you kilt quicker than a bite from a rattler. So he cut out."

Simon looked at Cole, who was half a foot taller than he was and outweighed him by a good fifty pounds. He found it hard to imagine someone so big being so shy. "No harm done. I'm just glad I didn't shoot him."

Jacob spat tobacco juice at a rail and hit it dead center. "Kilt many men have you, Mr. Ward?"

"Call me Simon. A few, yes. A while back slavers tried to steal my wife. I had to kill some of them to save her."

"You don't say?" Jacob winked at the younger Coyfields. "Hear that, boys? Even Yankees can be dangerous. You remember that. Even a rabbit will turn on you when it's cornered."

For the life of him, Simon Ward did not understand why the four men burst out laughing.

Chapter Four

Nate King's morning was a busy one.

He was up well before first light. His beautiful Shoshone wife, Winona, was curled on her side, raven tresses framing her lovely face. Nate pecked her lightly on the cheek before sliding from bed, then dressed in his buckskins, armed himself, and quietly snuck to the door so as not to awaken her or anyone else.

Evelyn and Zach were in their respective corners. Precious little Evelyn was an angel in repose. Zach snored lightly.

Louisa May Clark slept near the table, bundled in quilts and blankets, only her nose poking out.

There was just the one bed. The cabin was not spacious enough to accommodate more. Evelyn and Zach had been sleeping on the floor since they were toddlers. Sleeping comfortably, too, thanks to thick quilts Winona crafted, quilts as soft and warm as down-filled mattresses.

The door creaked as it was opened and closed. At that altitude the morning air was chill enough for Nate to see his breath. The stallion was not keen on being roused so early, and Nate had to pull it from the corral. Once it was saddled and mounted, he rode eastward to the lake. The ducks and geese that called it home were out in the middle, floating quietly. Eight or nine deer were drinking close to heavy cover; they ran off when Nate appeared. He circled around to the far side, then climbed a narrow trail that led to the main pass into the valley.

He dismounted, tied the stallion, and climbed higher. A winding track brought him to a rocky escarpment affording a magnificent vista of not only the valley but all the surrounding mountains, including mighty Longs Peak. Between his valley and Longs Peak lay another valley, claimed by his good friends the Wards.

Seated on a flat slab, Nate scoured his domain for signs of smoke or a telltale pinpoint of light. His instincts told him that whoever had shot at him was still in the area. The two strangers were a threat to his family, and he was determined to eliminate that threat as soon as possible.

Nate was a peaceable man by nature. He had no special fondness for killing, but he would kill without hesitation or qualms when his loved ones were endangered. Bitter experience had taught him the folly of offering the hand of friendship to those who would chop it off.

He sat on the slab until a golden sun pushed above the eastern horizon. With the advent of a new day the forest below resounded to the warbling of countless birds. Creatures that had hidden in their burrows and dens to elude the legion of nighttime predators now came boldly into the light to enjoy their appointed time on earth. Squirrels, chipmunks, marmots, deer, and more appeared in staggering numbers.

Nate returned to the pass to check for hoofprints. He found no evidence the pair had been through it. Another trail led into the valley from the north, but the only one who knew that trail existed was Shakespeare McNair, the man he thought of more as a father than a friend. The odds were slim that anyone else had discovered the route.

Nate suspected the pair had come in through a small pass to the southwest. If so, that did not bode well for the Wards. To reach it, the two men had to pass through the valley Simon and Felicity had laid claim to.

Deeply troubled, Nate trotted to the lake. A thorough search of the shore failed to turn up tracks other than those belonging to his own stock. He was about to go into the pines when he heard the drum of hoofs and down the trail from the cabin came his son.

Zach King was peeved his father had not seen fit to ask him to tag along. He wasn't a boy anymore. He could take care of himself, as the coup he had counted proved. So when he caught up to the black stallion, the first thing he said was, "Let me guess. You didn't want me slowing you down? Or you were afraid I'd get myself killed if we met up with those vermin who shot at you?"

Nate had to remind himself that at Zach's age he had been just as hot-tempered. "Good morning to you, too, son."

Zach frowned. His pa had a way of putting him in his place that grated on his nerves. "Morning. But don't change the subject. I'm a warrior now, Pa. I'd like it if you treated me as one."

"Why do you think I left you at the cabin?" Nate responded. "I was counting on you to watch out for your ma and the girls."

"Oh," Zach felt foolish. "Sorry. I should have known better."

"Now that you're here, you might as well come with me. Two sets of eyes are better than one."

Nate threaded in among the trees, making for a belt of grass that fringed the valley's southern edge. Sometimes, he mused, his son was so like him it was uncanny. Watching Zach grow up was like watching himself grow up all over again. Only, there were crucial differences. Differences that had molded Zach's character in unforeseen ways. Differences that gave Nate cause for concern.

New York City and the Rockies were literally worlds apart, as alien from each other as the earth from the moon. Nate's childhood had been spent in the biggest city in North America; Zach's had been spent in one of the most remote and wild areas on the continent. Nate's days had consisted of going to school to learn his ABCs; at the same age, Zach had been learning how to track and hunt, and when need be, how to kill. Nate had spent his free time with childhood friends, playing typical kid games; Zach was only among boys his own age in the summer when the family stayed with the Shoshones, and the games the boys played always had to do with honing skills that would serve them well as warriors.

Where Nate learned the Ten Commandments and the Golden Rule, Zach learned to distrust whites and to look on most other Indian tribes as his mortal enemies. Where Nate had never slain another human as a child, never even *thought* of doing so until he was a grown man, Zach had made his first kill while still a small boy and now accepted killing as part and parcel of everyday life. Where Nate's childhood had been civilized and tame, Zach's had been swamped in savagery.

Most troubling of all was Zach's hatred of whites. Given the bigotry the boy had suffered, Nate could understand why. But the knowledge did not make the hatred any easier to bear.

Then along came Louisa May Clark. It was said that the surest cure for hate was love, and Nate witnessed the miracle firsthand. Impossibly, his son was smitten, and almost immediately Zach changed. The hatred that had ruled Zach's life these past few years dwindled, melting like butter under a hot sun. His son smiled more, laughed more, enjoyed life more. Nate owed the girl a debt he could never repay.

''She's not a girl, Pa.''

''What?'' Nate looked up, thinking his son had somehow read his mind.

''A minute ago you called Lou a girl. She's not. She's a woman.''

''Well, she is only sixteen . . .''

"So? What does that have to do with anything? We both know Shoshone women her age who have husbands and sprouts. Lou is old enough to marry if she wants. If someone were interested, that is."

Nate had an inkling where the conversation would lead. He prudently stayed silent.

"Take me, for example. I care for her, Pa. I care for her a lot. I've never met anyone like her, and I can't stand to think that you might make her go back to St. Louis to be with her kin." Zach had been working up to this for days. He'd thought it would be hard to bare his soul, and he'd been right. His parents always encouraged him to come to them when he was troubled, but there were certain things a person would rather keep to himself.

"I just want to do what's best for her," Nate said. "Unless you expect her to live with us the rest of her life."

"No. I want her to live with me."

Nate drew rein. "Do you realize what you're saying?"

Zach squared his shoulders. "Yes, I reckon I do, Pa. I'm telling you that I love her. I'm telling you that I want to marry her. I want to do like you've done with Ma. Have a place of our own where we can raise a family." Now that Zach had started to unburden himself, he was afraid to stop for fear he wouldn't get it all out. "The Wards have that valley to the south, but what about the next one down? It's got water and some grass for forage. You could help me build a cabin. We'd have it done by winter if Simon helps, and Scott Kendall if he gets back. By next spring you could even be a grandpa. What do you say?"

To say Nate was dumbfounded would be the understatement of the century.

Zach took his father's silence as a sign of disapproval. "I know what you're thinking. That Lou and I are too young. That maybe I don't really love her. Maybe I only think I do. But you're wrong, Pa. I love her with all my heart. So what if we've only known each other a short while? How long did you know Ma before you knew you were in love with her?''

Nate recollected the details of his own courtship, such as it was. As he recalled, they had been thrown together more by circumstance than mutual design.

''Say something, will you?'' Zach fidgeted, regretting he had let it slip, thinking it might have been best to wait awhile and to do so with his mother present. He could usually count on her for moral support. His father was always stricter, always sterner. ''Are you mad? Upset? Shocked?''

''No, son. Your mother and I have seen this coming.''

''You have?''

Nate chuckled. Children, even at Zach's age, thought they could pull the wool over their parents' eyes. They never saw how transparent they were. For example, as a boy Zach liked to sneak sweetcakes from the pantry. Nate and Winona always caught on, which never ceased to astonish him. Zach figured they were spying on him. But it was the crumbs in his clothes and bedding that gave him away.

''So what do you say, Pa? Will you help build a cabin?''

''Not so fast,'' Nate answered. ''This is hardly the time or place to chaw it over. Let's wait until your mother and Lou can take part.''

Zach stiffened. He hadn't said anything to Lou yet. He preferred to have everything arranged, then ask her to be his wife. ''I'd be obliged if we could keep this between us. For the time being.''

''If that's what you want.'' Nate resumed the search for sign. ''We'll talk about it more when we get back.'' It would give him time to ponder, to come up with a thousand and one reasons why Zach and Lou should put it off, why the two of them shouldn't get hitched at their tender ages. Not that they would listen. They had an even better reason why they *should* get married. They were in love.

Besides that, Nate reflected, Zach wasn't much younger

than Simon and Felicity Ward, and look at how well they were doing.

Mabel Coyfield pushed back her plate. "I declare, missy. You make the best-tastin' flapjacks I ever did eat. I'm plumb full."

Felicity Ward wiped a hand across her sweaty brow, then blew a puff of air at a stray wisp of hair hanging clear down to her chin. For the past two hours she had slaved at the stove making enough food to feed their guests. The Coyfields were bottomless pits. Mabel alone ate five helpings. Jacob outdid her by two. Practically all the flour Felicity had was gone, along with most of her prized maple syrup, which she had hoarded for special occasions.

Mabel glanced at her oldest son, Cole. "Ain't she a fine cook, boy? She'd make any man happy, wouldn't she?"

Felicity had lost track of the number of times the mother had made similar comments, always to Cole. She did not know what to make of it, but she did know she didn't like it. "Anyone else still hungry? Speak right up."

No one was. Mabel, Jacob, and Samuel were at the table. Cindy Lou had claimed the rocking chair. The rest were sprawled at various spots on the floor, Mary Beth seated cross-legged like a boy. She had found a silver of wood and was picking at her teeth.

Simon Ward would be glad to see the clan go. They were nice enough in their crude way, but he didn't care for the insolent looks the sons gave him or how Cindy Lou winked at him every so often. As for the parents, Samuel hardly said ten words the whole meal. Jacob was the talker of the family, and he had gone on and on about their travels west, about the "critters" they had seen and the Indians they had clashed with.

"I reckon that last bunch was Pawnees," the patriarch was now saying, between belches. "They tried to steal our mules, but we was too smart for 'em. We have this trick we learned back in the hills, in Georgia—''

"I thought you said you were from Arkansas?" Simon interrupted.

"Georgia was before Arkansas," Jacob said gruffly, then patted his bulging stomach and belched again. "Anyhow, we have this trick, see. We dig a shallow hole and one of us lies in it all night to watch the string. Covered with grass and weeds so no one can spot us. Works every time."

Samuel Coyfield smiled. "Got me two scalps that night."

"What?" Simon said. "You took their hair?"

Jacob had lifted his coffee cup and was staring into it as if the gallon he had already downed were not enough. "They'd've taken ours, friend. Ma's and the girls' and everybody's. Turnabout is fair play, eh? So we took theirs instead."

"I like that squaw's hair," Cindy Lou remarked.

The contents of Simon's stomach churned. "There was a woman with them? You scalped her too?"

Jacob shook his great moon of a head. "No, no. The squaw was another time. When we come on this small village. Not more than five or six tepees, there was. The menfolk were gone, off huntin' buffalo, I expect. So we did to 'em as they'd've done to any whites they found. We kilt all the women and children."

"You didn't."

"Hell, man. Lice breed more lice, don't they? What are you, an Injun lover? If'n you'd seen what those red devils do to white folks, you wouldn't be so pussy-kitten. I had me an uncle who was gutted like a fish by the Cherokees. And a neighbor of our'n was tied to a tree and used as a target for Seminole pigstickers. Turned ol' Walt into a pincushion, they did."

Simon resented the man more by the minute. "Not all Indians are vicious. If you run into any Shoshones, treat them decently. They've never harmed a white man. They like being our friends.''

Sam Coyfield's hawkish features curved downward. "Injuns are Injuns, mister. The only good ones are maggot bait.''

Mabel stirred. "Be nice, Samuel. Mr. Ward is a Yankee, remember? And Yankees don't think like regular folks.''

Simon resented being patronized. "I'm not the only one who likes the Shoshones, Mrs. Coyfield. Ask any trapper and he'll agree. The same with the Flatheads and the Nez Percé. They've gone out of their way to help the white man.''

Mabel's dark eyes twinkled. "If'n you say so, sugar. But then, we're new to these parts. We've got a lot to learn.''

"That you do,'' Simon stressed, garnering spiteful stares from several of the sons. Cole, in particular, was blatant about it.

Jacob Coyfield pushed his chair back and craned his neck. "Sure is a nice place you've got here, friend. Right cozy and warm. I bet that roof sure keeps out the rain, don't it? Have many leaks?''

"None at all,'' Simon said, thinking, *What a silly question.*

"You don't say? Ours back to home leaked something awful.''

"Why didn't you fix it?''

Jacob's flabby jowls lowered. "You mean, climb up on top and plug the holes?''

"That'd be work,'' Samuel remarked.

Simon looked from one to the other. "So?''

It was Cole who answered. "Workin' around the house is for womenfolk, Yankee. Men do the huntin' and skinnin' and fightin' and such. Any fool knows that.''

"Keep your insults to yourself,'' Simon bristled.

Mabel intervened again. "Now, now, Cole. There's no call to be lookin' down your nose at our host. Yankees have different notions about work than we do. I hear tell that their menfolk even help the womenfolk wash and dry dishes.''

Cole, Jess, Tinder, and Bo roared. Cindy Lou and Mary Beth cackled. Even Jacob and Samuel enjoyed a merry laugh.

Simon carried his plate to the counter so they would not see how angry he had become. He had met southerners before, but never any who behaved like the Coyfields. He couldn't wait for them to leave.

Felicity wiped her hands on her apron. "How about if you ladies help me clean up while the men step outside and have a smoke?" She was anxious to get them out of her house and see them on their way, and intuition told her Simon felt the same.

"What's wrong with smokin' inside?" Jacob asked.

Mabel smacked him on the arm. "Where are your manners, Pa? Do as the lady wants. Me and the girls will take care of things in here. You understand? You take your business outside."

Jacob grinned. "I savvy, Ma. Don't you fret." Rising, he nodded at the four bearded bears. "Didn't you hear? Mosey your lazy hind ends outdoors."

Simon dipped his plate in the bucket and ran a washcloth over it. The Coyfields be hanged! It didn't make him less of a man because he helped his wife do chores. When the last of the men trudged by, he set the plate down and moved close enough to Felicity to say under his breath, "Come up with an excuse to get rid of them. Much more of this and I'll use language you've never heard me use before."

Felicity grinned, then tweaked his cheek. "They'll be leaving soon, I'm sure," she whispered. "Another hour won't kill you."

"Want to bet?"

Simon headed out. He hesitated at the gun rack, debating whether to take his rifle, then walked on without it. He might be tempted to shoot one of them.

The Coyfields were lounging at their ease, Jacob and Samuel straddling a log that bordered the flower garden.

"Be careful of my wife's flowers," Simon cautioned. Felicity had invested countless hours digging and planting and nurturing the sprouts.

"Flowers?" Jacob repeated, and glanced down at where his boot heel ground a fragile stem into the dirt. "Oh. Sorry, friend. Land sakes, I know how fussy women can be about plants. Ma had this rose she was powerful fond of. The cat pissed on it one day, so she shot him dead."

Samuel was scratching an armpit. "Tell me, Yankee. How many neighbors you got hereabouts? Other than that big feller to the north."

Simon leaned against the cabin. "You know Nate King? He's one of the best friends I've ever had. If not for him, Felicity and I would have died long ago." Simon rapped on the wall. "Nate and Shakespeare McNair helped us build this cabin. To be honest, they did most of the work. It's a wonder what those two can do. Jacks-of-all-trades, you'd call them."

Jacob was treating himself to another mouthful of chewing tobacco. "McNair? Who's he? Where's he live?"

"About twenty-five miles north of Nate. Shakespeare has been in these mountains longer than anyone. They say he was here before Lewis and Clark came, that he was one of the first whites to set foot in the Rockies."

"An old guy, then?" Jacob said, and grinned at his brother.

"You wouldn't call him that if you saw him. He's stronger than most men half his age and has more energy than your whole family combined. Where he gets it from is beyond me. I'll count myself blessed if I live half as long as he has."

"Any other folks hereabouts?" Samuel asked.

Simon wondered why the brother was suddenly so interested in how many neighbors he had. "That's about all. It isn't like back in the States. I doubt there are ten homesteads like ours in the entire Rockies. A couple of dozen trappers live with Indians, but they're scattered with the tribes."

Jacob chewed loudly. "It's like I said it'd be, brother. White folks are as scarce as hen's teeth in these parts."

Cole grunted like a bear rooting for grubs. "Then what are we waitin' for, Pa? Why don't we get it over with? I'm mighty tired of playin' games."

Simon stretched. The meal had made him sluggish. A nice long nap was in order, once he disposed of his visitors. "Get what over with?" he idly asked.

"Oh, he's just a mite too eager to settle into a place of our own," Jacob answered, rising ponderously. Smiling, he walked up to Cole and cuffed him across the mouth. The younger man rocked on his haunches but did not lift a hand to defend himself. "How many times I got to tell you, boy? You speak when you're told to and not before. That mouth of yours is going to get you in a heap of trouble if'n you ain't careful."

"Sorry, Pa," Cole said meekly.

Samuel did not seem the least bit interested in the dispute between father and son. "Tell me, Ward. Many people besides us have stopped by your place?"

"Oh, mountain men from time to time. Maybe one a month, on average."

"Any of 'em you know real well? Good friends, like?"

"Nate and Shakespeare are my only real friends. Oh, and Scott Kendall. I forgot about him. He has a cabin seven miles away, but right now he's in Massachusetts. His wife likes to go back every other year or so to visit their families."

Jacob was waddling to the log. "Wise woman. Nothing is more important than kin. To me and mine, blood is everything. We stand by one another no matter what. It's us against the world, and we aim to come out on top."

"I wouldn't say the whole world is out to get you—" Simon began.

"You ain't from the hills," Jacob said. "You don't know what life there is like." He spat into the flowers. "The Coyfields have always been as close as peas in a pod. When one of us needs help, the rest are right there. When one of us is in danger, we take it as if we're all in danger. When killin' needs doing, we do it as a family. Why, even when we marry, we almost always marry someone from inside the clan. Mabel, in fact, is my sister.''

Simon was appalled to his core. "You married your own sister? Isn't that against the law?''

"We don't take no stock by man's laws,'' Jacob said, offended. "The only laws we obey are the ones we make our own selves. That's been the Coyfield way for as long as there have been Coyfields, and it will go on being our way till the end of creation.''

Simon glanced at Cole and Jess. "Do you mean to tell me that one of them will be forced to marry Cindy Lou or Mary Beth?''

"Not hardly, mister,'' Cole said testily.

Jacob elaborated. "Every now and again we like to bring new blood into the line. To keep it healthy, like when raisin' cows or some such. Cole has a hankerin' after a lady who ain't a Coyfield. And from what I saw, she'll make a fine addition.''

"He has to go all the way back to Arkansas for his bride?'' Simon said, amused. Hadn't it occurred to the buffoon to ask the woman *before* the clan left?

Cole rose to his feet. Jacob motioned, but Cole paid him no mind. "Hell no, mister. All I got to do is walk through that door. The woman I'm fixin' to take for my own is your wife.''

Chapter Five

Louisa May Clark was seated on a boulder beside the lake. Her knees were tucked to her chest, her arms wrapped around her legs, and she was in heaven. To her, the lake was gorgeous, the valley was gorgeous, the Rockies were gorgeous. The air had a tingle to it she had never noticed before. The water was bluer, the trees and grass were greener. The earth was incredibly rich; life itself was incredibly wonderful. It was as if she saw everything through whole new eyes.

Lou wasn't fooling herself. She knew why she felt so supremely alive. Zachary King had claimed her heart, and somehow, in the bargain, heightened her senses to a level she had never experienced. She was happy and content for the first time since her mother died, and she didn't want it to end.

But an ominous cloud loomed on her horizon. Just that morning, Winona had asked her for what had to be the fiftieth time what she intended to do with her life. Did she want to go back to St. Louis? Would she rather go to Ohio? Did she have relatives who would put her up? What, exactly, were her plans?

Lou had hedged, as usual. She had no plans other than the one her heart dictated: to marry Stalking Coyote. Beyond that, she really didn't care. So long as she was with him, where they lived or what they did were of no consequence.

It was ironic, Lou thought. A few short weeks before she had been in misery, crushed by the loss of her father. She had been mad at the unfairness of it all, at having no one left who truly cared for her, at being thrown on her own in the middle of the vast wilderness, at being at the end of her tether with no hope for the future. Then Zach came into her life and everything changed. Just like that. One day she was in deep despair, the next she had met the man she wanted to live with for the rest of her days.

Who would have thought such a thing could happen?

Lou had learned an important lesson. A person's life could change with the snap of a finger. Nothing was graven in stone. Fortune, romance, life itself, hung by thin threads. People were puppets, and some higher power was pulling the strings that put them in motion. A higher power that, until she met Zach, had seemed to be cruel and fickle. Now she wasn't so sure.

The same God that had allowed her father to be brutally slain had brought Zach and her together. Was the one act meant to balance out the other? Were both mere happenstance? Random events? Or was there a purpose to all she had gone through? Was her life, as her minister in Ohio liked to say, part of some mysterious Divine Plan?

Lou had no idea. It was all too much for her to fathom. What she did know was that she loved Zach as she had never loved anyone, and the idea of losing him filled her with terror. She didn't think she could bear it. She would rather die.

If only Zach would come out and voice his feelings. If only he would confirm how he felt and give her some idea of what he wanted to do about it.

Then, as if in answer to her plea, the object of her heartfelt desire appeared at the mouth of the trail to the cabin.

Zach smiled and waved. The sun was high in the sky, well past its apex. Hooking his thumbs in his belt, he sauntered along the rocky shore. Outwardly he put on a show of being calm but butterflies fluttered in his belly and his heart was beating as if he had just run a mile. "Howdy, Louisa. Ma told me I'd find you here."

Lou lowered her legs. "How did the search go? Find any sign of those men?"

"Some old tracks, is all. Pa went to the pass that links our valley to the one the Wards live in. We found where two riders headed this way about a week ago. Pa figures they've been spying on us all that time."

"Why? What are they up to?"

"Pa doesn't rightly know. If they were meaning to harm us, you'd think they'd have done so by now."

"They took a shot at your father," Lou pointed out.

"Because he was after them." Zach roosted on a boulder next to hers. "Maybe if he'd let them be, they wouldn't have tried to kill him." He shrugged. "We just don't know what to make of it. But Pa's determined to find them and learn what they're up to."

Lou gazed at the dense woodland, wondering if the men were watching them that very minute.

"Ma's worried about the Wards. She thinks Pa and her ought to ride over there and see if they're all right."

"Will we be going along?"

"I don't know yet. I told them we'd keep an eye on our place while they're gone. Ma doesn't much like the idea. Pa is straddling the fence. He thinks those polecats might be after our horses, or maybe they're waiting for a chance to break into the cabin and rob us blind." Zach snickered. "Not that we have all that much worth stealing. A few guns and plews and clothes. Hardly worth the bother."

"I wouldn't mind staying here with you," Lou said. Zach and she would be alone for the first time since they got there. Truly alone. To do whatever they pleased. Warmth gushed through her at the prospect.

"Pa said he'd let us know at supper. Ma wants to leave

YES!

Sign me up for the Leisure Western Book Club
and send my FOUR FREE BOOKS! If I choose to stay
in the club, I will pay only $14.00* each month,
a savings of $9.96!

NAME: _____

ADDRESS: _____

_____

TELEPHONE: _____

E-MAIL: _____

☐ I WANT TO PAY BY CREDIT CARD.

☐ VISA   ☐ MasterCard   ☐ DISCOVER

ACCOUNT #: _____

EXPIRATION DATE: _____

SIGNATURE: _____

Send this card along with $2.00 shipping & handling to:

**Leisure Western Book Club
20 Academy Street
Norwalk, CT 06850-4032**

Or fax (must include credit card information!) to: 610.995.9274.
You can also sign up online at www.dorchesterpub.com.

*Plus $2.00 for shipping. Offer open to residents of the U.S. and Canada only.
Canadian residents please call 1.800.481.9191 for pricing information.

If under 18, a parent or guardian must sign. Terms, prices and conditions subject to change. Subscription subject
to acceptance. Dorchester Publishing reserves the right to reject any order or cancel any subscription.

JOIN NOW!

in the morning. Felicity and her have gotten real close, and Ma's fretting something awful.''

"Anything else?"

Zach almost said "No." But that would be a lie. He had come to the lake for the express purpose of airing his feelings and learning how she felt about the two of them maybe living together. The talk with his father had made him realize it was long overdue. Asking his pa to help build a cabin was putting the cart before the horse. First, he had to find out if she considered him as much a part of her life as he considered her a part of his. But when he glanced around, when he saw her sparkling eyes and smooth cheeks and cherry-red lips, he heard himself say, "Nice day, isn't it?"

"Nicest ever."

Zach tore his gaze from her in order to concentrate. "We get a lot of nice days like this up here."

"My father used to call the mountains God's footstools. They're beautiful."

"Not half as beautiful as you."

"Thank you."

"Lou—?"

"Yes?"

Zach gripped the boulder so hard, his knuckles were white. Twisting, he licked his dry lips. "We've grown pretty close, haven't we?"

"You might say that." Lou could barely hear him for the din her heart was making. Something important was about to happen. She could feel it in her blood. "I've never been close to anyone in the way I've been close to you." Having admitted how brazen she had been, she blushed.

Instead of getting to the point, Zach stalled. "Pa used to tell me that one day I'd like kissing girls. I knew better. Girls never interested me. I was never going to kiss one. Never going to marry one. I'd have me a dog and a horse and that was all I'd need."

"I felt pretty much the same about boys. Only, I was going to have a cat."

"I did have a dog once. His name was Samson. Lordy, he was big. He could hold his own against panthers and bears. But Apaches killed him on a visit to Santa Fe. I was so sad, I cried and cried." Zach smiled fondly. "About a year or so later, on an elk hunt with my pa, I stumbled on Blaze, the wolf who saved you and me from that war party when we first met. He was just a cub back then. We were always together until he took to spending more time with his own kind. And I love you."

Lou was bending to pick up a stone to chuck into the water. "What?" She was not sure she had heard what she thought she had heard.

Zach was aghast at his stupidity. He had intended to lead up to it slowly, not spit it out as if it were a sour berry. What must she think? He had to own up to it, come what may. "I love you, Lou. I reckon you already know that."

Louisa forgot about the stone. Without looking at him, she said, "I love you too, Stalking Coyote."

Out on the lake waterfowl were making a racket. Ducks quacked and fluttered their wings. Geese honked noisily. In the forest jays squawked, sparrows chirped, and robins twittered. Squirrels were chattering, chipmunks were chittering. One moment, Zach and Lou heard all these sounds with striking clarity; the next their whole world went abruptly silent. It wasn't that the animals stopped singing or chattering; Zach and Lou simply stopped hearing them.

Lou had ears only for Stalking Coyote. She hung on his next words with bated breath, her fingers trembling ever so slightly.

Zach felt as if a great wind were rushing through his ears. His chest was constricted and his palms were hot enough to fry eggs on. Swallowing hard, he said, "I'm probably being too forward by saying this, but I can't abide the thought of you leaving us. Ma and Pa keep talking about you going back to the States. I'd rather you didn't. I'd be right pleased if you'd stay here with us. With me.''

Lou shifted to face him.

''I'm not much to look at and I'm not the smartest coon who ever lived. But I'm not a lazy no-accounts who'd let his woman starve. I know how to provide for a family. I'd make a passable husband.''

''Are you asking me to marry you?''

Zach's cheeks were aflame. Yes, he was asking that very thing. Only, he had to say it plain, to come right out with the question. It was on the tip of his tongue. He was *that* close. And suddenly, beyond her, deep in the depths of the tall trees, a two-legged shape materialized. Zach couldn't say if it had been there all along and he had just spotted it, or the man had edged into the open for a better look-see. The instant Zach saw him, the man wheeled and ran.

''Damn!''

Lou was shocked when the apple of her desire leaped up and sprinted toward the woods. She had been sure he was about to propose, and she had girded herself to answer. Now she jumped up, exclaiming, ''Stalking Coyote? What in tarnation?''

''It's one of those men! Fetch my pa!''

Lou did no such thing. The two strangers had tried to kill Nate, so it was unlikely they'd have any reservations about killing Nate's son. She raced after him.

Zach plunged into the undergrowth, his moccasins flying. Among the Shoshones he was accounted as exceptionally fleet of foot, and he proved it now by swiftly gaining on the fleeing figure. The man looked back once, revealing a hook nose and a bushy beard. Zach also saw a rifle, something Zach didn't have. He had left his at the cabin, thinking his two pistols were enough protection on a short walk to the lake. But he was not about to turn back. He would catch the coyote and further prove to his pa he was competent to be on his own—as Lou's husband and protector.

It wouldn't be easy. The man was running faster, holding his own. Zach was hard-pressed to keep him in sight. With a hand on the butt of a flintlock at all times, Zach wound through the trees. He was seldom able to run in a straight line for more than a dozen yards thanks to all the obstacles. To further narrow the gap he hurtled over a log, then crashed through a thicket.

Without warning the figure vanished.

Zach slowed, wary of a ruse. Drawing the flintlock, he advanced a stone's throw past the spot where he had last seen the stranger. There were no tracks, nothing. He turned to backtrack, and in the split second he did, he recognized his blunder. For in an instant the man was upon him.

Zach spun, but he was too slow by half. The man had launched himself into the air. As Zach brought up the pistol, the man slammed into him with the force of a battering ram.

Simon Ward looked at each of the Coyfields in turn, waiting for them to laugh. He thought Cole's crude comment had been made in jest, but when none of them so much as cracked a grin and he saw Jacob give the oldest son a resentful glance, a terrible premonition came over him. Snapping erect, he declared, "That does it. I've tried to be civil. But this is the last straw. I want all of you to leave."

None of the Coyfields moved.

Simon placed each hand on a pistol. "Did you hear me? I want you to take your women and get the hell out of here."

Jacob Coyfield sighed, then pointed a thick finger at Cole. "See what your loose tongue has done? Gone and set him off. And we wanted this to go without a hitch."

Simon's irritation mounted. "Wanted what to go without a hitch? If you really believe your son can have my wife, you're a lunatic. Mount up and ride out."

"We can't do that, friend," Jacob said. "Much as it pains me to say so, we've taken a shine to your place. This cabin will make a fine home. There's plenty of game and water. Everything a feller could want right at his fingertips. So we're movin' in and you're movin' out."

Anger bordering on rage seized Simon. Training a flintlock on Jacob and another on Samuel, he announced, "If you're not on your way out of here within one minute, I'll shoot you both. So help me God."

Samuel extended a palm. "Now, you just hold on, friend. Don't do anything rash. We'll sort this out soon enough."

"I'm not your friend and I never will be!" Simon fumed, furious that they sat there like bumps on a log, showing no fear of him or his guns. "And there's nothing to sort out. Get up and *go*!"

"Now, Pa?" Cole asked.

"Not yet, boy. Ain't you got the brains of a turnip? You'll know when it's time."

At that exact instant, inside the cabin a commotion arose. A plate shattered with a resounding crash. A chair upended. There was a low cry, then Felicity called out, "Simon! Simon! Help me!"

Automatically, Simon whirled. He glimpsed his wife locked in a struggle with Cindy Lou and Mary Beth. He started to rush to her aid when iron hands seized him and he was thrown to the ground. He swung out, his right pistol connecting with a bearded face. Heavy bodies pinned him. His arms were violently pressed flat, his pistols rendered useless. A boot stomped onto his right hand, lancing pain clear up his arm. He gritted his teeth to keep from crying out, then kicked at a pair of stout legs. One of the sons—was it Bo?—backed off, doubled in agony.

"Hold him, you damn whelps!" Samuel shouted.

"Can't the four of you whip a measly Yankee?" Jacob demanded.

Hands gripped Simon's ankles. He was unable to move, except for his neck, which he craned to see into the cabin. His blood ran cold. Mabel Coyfield had the sharp edge of a butcher knife pressed against his wife's tender throat. "No! Leave her alone, you bitch!"

Simon never saw Jacob kick him. But he felt the blow on his left cheek, felt it down to his toes. Anguish ripped him, as much emotional as physical. Warm drops of blood trickled down over his jaw.

"Don't be talkin' to my missus like that, Yank," Jacob said harshly. "She's got her flaws, but as womenfolk go she don't give me much cause to complain. It was her idea to claim this valley for our own. A right smart idea it was, too."

Simon couldn't care less about Mabel Coyfield. His sole interest was his wife. Felicity was being ushered outside, each of the daughters holding an arm. "Are you all right?" he asked, his numb tongue and puffy cheek distorting the words.

"I'm unharmed," Felicity responded. Except for a few bruises—and the hurt she felt inside, the regret at being so open and friendly when her intuition warned her something was amiss—that was true. What was it Winona King once said? "You can never let your guard down around strangers. They must earn your trust. Until they do, keep a weapon handy and have eyes in the back of your head."

Simon felt fingers prying at his, seeking to strip him of the pistols. He attempted to twist his arm to shoot and nearly screeched when someone gave his wrist a vicious wrench.

"Let go of the guns, Yankee," Cole said, hiking a foot, "or I'll kick your teeth in and make you eat 'em."

Felicity tried to break free, but the two daughters were easily her match. "Do as he says, Simon. We don't want to give them cause to do more than they already have."

Mabel Coyfield still held the butcher knife. "Oh, you needn't worry about yourself, dearie. My boy Cole has his sights set on you. But your husband here . . ." She stood over Simon and motioned as if hacking meat to bits.

"No! You can't!" Felicity attempted to take a step, but Cindy Lou and Mary Beth held her fast. Tears of outrage dampened her eyes, and she blinked to clear her vision. Something else Winona had told her sprung unbidden into her mind: *"When you are in danger, try to stay calm. Lose your head and you lose your life."*

"Maybe we shouldn't do it here, Ma," Jacob was saying. "It's liable to upset Cole's new gal something awful."

"Just so it gets done proper," Mabel said. "Bury him good and deep so the varmints don't dig him up like they did that last feller. We wouldn't want anyone to find the grave. Then we'd have to light a shuck again, and I'm mighty tired of being on the run. The girls and me are sick to death of sleepin' on the ground like dogs."

Jess Coyfield, who had a jagged scar above his left eye, glanced at his mother. "That body business weren't my fault, Ma. I told Cole and Hap they didn't bury that old codger far enough down, but they wouldn't listen. What could I do?"

Mabel turned with surprising speed for someone her size and slapped her youngest. "Quit your tattlin'. What's done is done. We shook the law, didn't we? We're safe, and we've got us a new home. All's well that ends well."

Felicity had gleaned enough to say, "You've done this before, haven't you? Is this why you had to leave Arkansas? Someone caught on? It had nothing to do with a feud, did it?"

"Oh, there was a feud, all right. The McErny clan drove us out of Georgia with our tails between our legs. We ended up in Arkansas. It didn't seem right we'd have to start over with nothin' but the clothes on our backs, so we took a farmer's house for our own. Told folks he'd sold it to us. But some people just won't believe you even when you swear on a stack of Bibles. A few got suspicious, started nosin' around, and found the bodies of the farmer and his family." Mabel grinned and gestured. "Here we are."

"You're unspeakably evil," Felicity said.

"We just do what we have to in order to survive, dearie. Don't take it personal."

Simon had been listening so intently, he forgot about Cole. A piercing pang in his shoulder reminded him.

"For the last time, Yank. Let go of the pistols."

What else could Simon do? With great reluctance he relaxed his grip and both flintlocks were immediately snatched from his grasp. Tinder and Bo, Samuel's boys, hauled him to his feet and Tinder looped a forearm around his neck.

"So you won't get frisky."

Samuel Coyfield was fingering the hilt of his own knife. "Let's take him off and get it over with. I'd like to take a nap later, then sit a spell by the fireplace and whittle. I don't want to have to get up and go out again."

Simon and Felicity looked into each other's eyes. Felicity, clutching at straws, quickly said, "Kill my husband and it will be Arkansas all over again. Our neighbors are due by soon. Nate King won't be fooled into thinking we've sold out, even if you hide me until he's gone. He'll come back with a small army of trappers and Shoshones and make you pay for your crimes."

Jacob and several of the sons chortled. "Think so, do you, sugar? Well, I'll have you know we've already thought of that. My son Hap and Samuel's son Vin have been spyin' on Mr. King for the better part of a week. Same as we've been spyin' on you. Soon as I send 'em word that we have everything under control here, they're to rub out King and his family. Cole and you will move into the King cabin. You'll have a place all your own. See? We're not as heartless as you make us out to be."

Felicity racked her brain. "You think you have everything figured out, don't you? But you're wrong. I'll bet you didn't know Nate King's wife is Shoshone. That he's an adopted Shoshone. That her people pay them regular visits. The tribe will never believe they up and left.''

''So? Nice bluff, but your husband done told us the Shoshones are the friendliest Injuns in all creation. They've never harmed a white man.''

Simon interjected, ''There's always a first time. Especially if you've killed one of their people. And don't forget. Nate King is widely known and widely respected. He gets a lot more visitors than we do. If the Shoshones don't get you, the mountain men will. They tend to stick together, just like your clan.''

Jacob spat tobacco juice on Simon's left foot. ''It won't work, friend. We have our minds made up.''

Mabel was scratching her triple chin with the tip of the butcher knife. ''Hold on, Pa. The damn city boy might have a point. The Kings have been here a lot longer. Maybe wipin' them out ain't such a good idea.''

Cole took exception. ''But you said I could have my own place, Ma. You said. Me and the filly here. Just the two of us. You promised. You did.''

''Hush!'' Mabel hissed. ''You're worse than Jess.'' She gnawed on her fleshy lower lip a bit. ''I think we should play it safe. We'll hold off on killin' the Kings, and on buryin' this Yankee, until we've talked it over. There has to be a way to do this without havin' the stinkin' Shoshones and trappers down on our heads. There just has to.''

That ended the discussion. Cindy Lou and Mary Beth were ordered to take Felicity back inside. The boys were instructed what to do with Simon, and five minutes later Simon found himself being staked out in the high grass. Cole trained a pistol on him while Jess, Tinder, and Bo pounded long picket pins into the ground, then tied him spread-eagled.

''I want you to know something, Yankee,'' Cole said when they were done. ''I'm lookin' forward to makin' wolf

73

meat of you. Almost as much as I'm lookin' forward to gettin' my paws on that female of yours. When I'm done with her, she won't miss you one little bit.''

Simon had never hated anyone as much as he hated Cole Coyfield. ''Touch her and you'll die. Each and every one of you.''

Jess laughed. ''You've got it backwards, mister. You're the one who's going to be worm food before too long.''

Both sets of brothers departed. Simon tested the ropes around his wrists and ankles. They were so tight, he couldn't move his limbs. Stretching his neck, he sought to sink his teeth into the knots, but they were well out of reach. He was totally helpless, at the mercy of the Coyfields. Or whatever else might happen by.

Simon tried not to think of his darling Felicity, alone in the cabin with the clan of cutthroats. He couldn't bear to picture Cole's filthy hands on her. His only hope was to pray someone else came along. He would call out, warn them, urge them to reach Nate King and enlist help.

Simon had never been an advocate of scalping, but he would love to see Coyfield scalps adorning a Shoshone lodge or two.

A shadow fell across him. Cole Coyfield smirked and sank onto a knee. In Cole's hand was one of the washcloths Felicity had brought all the way from Boston. ''Ma sends her regards. She sent me to gag you.''

Chapter Six

Zachary King fought like a wildcat against a bear, pitting his wiry sinews and agility against his bearded adversary's greater bulk and raw power. The man had bowled him over and was astride his chest, a hand clamped on Zach's wrist to hold the pistol at bay while the other hand sought to bury a gleaming blade in Zach's chest. Zach had his own fingers locked around the man's arm to prevent the knife from descending, but his attacker had the advantage of being on top and outweighed him by a good fifty pounds. Inch by inch the knife dipped ever closer. In another few seconds the unyielding steel would embed itself.

Straining every muscle, Zach heaved upward, seeking to throw the man off. But his foe wouldn't budge. Zach's next gambit was to sweep a knee up into the skulker's back, once, twice, three times. At the third blow, the man snarled like a beast and shifted forward to avoid being kneed again.

For a few moments the stranger was off balance. Zach capitalized by heaving upward again and succeeded in partially bucking the man off. It enabled Zach to twist onto his side and gain more leverage. The knife, though, was a finger's width from Zach's buckskin shirt. He applied all the strength in his shoulders and arms to stave off the inevitable.

The man hissed like a serpent, spittle flecking his beard, his eyes pools of raving bloodlust. A vein on his temple bulged as he brought his entire weight to bear.

It was then that Louisa caught up with them. She had a

pistol out and cocked. Planting herself, she pointed it. "That's enough! Get off him! Or by all that's holy, I'll shoot!"

The man glanced up.

So did Zach. He saw Louisa eight feet away, then spotted someone else, off to the left of her. Fright almost paralyzed his tongue. "Lou! Look out! There's the other one!"

Louisa rotated, the motion saving her life. A rifle boomed. A lead ball that would have torn through her brain instead missed by a fraction, buzzing past her ear. She snapped off a shot of her own, but she was stumbling sideways and missed.

The man who had fired was on horseback, the reins to another horse across his leg. He snatched them up while spurring his mount forward. Both horses bore down on Lou like stampeding buffalo. She had to fling herself into brambles to avoid being trampled.

Meanwhile, the stocky man on top of Zach jumped to his feet. He kicked at Zach's face, but Zach rolled out of harm's way. A long bound brought the man to the riderless mount as it flashed past. Gripping the saddle horn, he swung onto the saddle. Both riders bent low and raced into the trees.

Zach surged erect and took hasty aim. Unfortunately, limbs and trunks intervened. He would waste the shot. Giving chase was his only recourse, but his horse was at the cabin. By the time he got there and back, the pair would be long gone. Stamping a foot at being thwarted, he tensed when a warm hand was placed on his neck.

"Are you all right?"

"I'm mad enough to chew rocks and spit pebbles." Zach lowered his pistol and shoved it under his belt.

Lou was the opposite. She was overjoyed he was unhurt. Their peril had fanned the spark of her love into an inferno. She desired to embrace him, hold him close, smother him with fiery kisses. Instead, she simply said, "I was so afraid."

Misunderstanding, Zach replied, "There was no need to be. I'd never let anything happen to you." He faced her. She radiated love as the sun radiated light, the splendor of her gaze reminding him of the question he had been about to ask when the stranger appeared. He would have to ask it later, in a more romantic setting.

Lou was intensely disappointed when Stalking Coyote turned and began to scour the grass. She had been sure he was going to take up where they had left off. "What are you looking for?"

"The man's rifle. I think he had one when I first saw him. He must have set it down so he could kill me with the knife. Less noise that way. Pa wouldn't hear and come on the run." Zach moved toward a tree near where the stranger had pounced. Propped against it on the other side was a fine Kentucky. "See? I knew it."

Lou didn't share his delight. She was too depressed. She would rather have the proposal. As he bent his legs toward the lake she fell into step beside him.

"Thank you for coming along when you did," Zach said. "I might have been a goner if you hadn't."

"I'd never let anything happen to you, either."

Zach grasped her hand. Presently, they came to the shore and he bore to the right. Seeing the boulders on which they had sat, he stopped. He had changed his mind. Why wait until later on? There was no time like the present. "Lou, there's something I need to say before . . ."

Louisa held her breath in anticipation. She would say "Yes"! She would hug him close and shout it at the top of her lungs so it echoed off the mountains. It would be a moment she treasured, one she would recall fondly in her twilight years. The day that changed her life forever.

But Zach never got to finish. A hail from the direction of the trail heralded the arrival of his father.

* * *

Nate King had heard a shot, grabbed his Hawken, and raced to learn the cause. Spying them as they stood hand in hand, he cupped a hand to his mouth. "What's going on? What was that shot about?"

Zach frowned, squeezed Lou's fingers gently, then ran to show his father the rifle and explain.

Nate wasted no time in hurrying back up the trail, giving instructions as he went. "No more straying from the cabin. Stay close at all times. I'm going after them while there's still plenty of daylight left, and I probably won't be back until late. Zach, I'm counting on you to keep watch. Climb on the roof and stay there until sunset. If they come back before I do, all of you get inside and bolt the door. You can hold off a small army if need be."

"Are you still fixing to leave in the morning to check on the Wards?"

"Need you ask?"

"Lou and I should stay here, then. Even if you get the pair who jumped us, someone has to protect our home."

"We'll see."

The stallion was still saddled, tied outside the corral. Nate mounted and was wheeling the big black around when the door opened and out rushed Winona.

"Where are you off to?"

"Zach will fill you in."

Nate lit out as if rabid wolves nipped at his heels. He had to cover a lot of ground quickly. Rather than waste precious time going to where Lou and his son had encountered the men, he angled to the north to cut their trail. Zach had said the pair rode westward. Assuming they were headed for the same general vicinity where he had heard them the night before, they had to cross a broad meadow a mile from the cabin. That was where he would pick up their trail.

In short order Nate was there. Four shaggy buffalo were grazing in the middle. An old bull placed himself between

Nate and the cows, snorting and grumbling like a cantankerous old man. Nate kept one eye on it as he searched along the meadow's west fringe. Freshly churned earth bore out his guesswork. The imprint of shod hoofs was plain as day.

"You're mine, you mangy bastards," Nate declared as he brought the stallion to a trot. The two men had been riding at a brisk walk. Apparently, they were convinced they had given Zach and Lou the slip and assumed they were safe.

For over half an hour Nate held to a pace that flecked the stallion with sweat. From a sawtooth spine dotted with firs he caught sight of the cutthroats who had dared invade his domain. They were taking their sweet time, jawing and grinning as if they didn't have a care in the world. They were about to learn differently.

Nate traveled in a loop to the south. The country was more open and there was greater risk of detection, but it also allowed him to go faster, to swing wide and get in front of the pair. He had a fair notion of the route they would take: an old game trail that snaked toward the mountain where they had taken a shot at him. They must have a camp secreted there.

Whoever they were, they had made a grave mistake. They failed to realize Nate knew every square foot of the valley. *Every single square foot.* He had lived there for almost twenty years, crisscrossed it from end to end and side to side. He had used every trail, poked into every nook and cranny, explored every slope. He had been through every stand of timber, he had climbed the surrounding peaks. He knew where each spring was, each meadow, each patch of wildflowers and berries. In short, he knew the valley as well as he knew the back of his own hand.

So it was child's play for Nate to get ahead of the interlopers, to reach a point where the game trail passed a rock outcropping, to tie the stallion and move along the side of the outcropping so he was in position when the dull thud of hoofs broke the stillness. Voices with a distinct southern twang preceded the duo.

"—wish we'd hear something. I can't figure what's takin' 'em so long."

"You never was a patient cuss, Vin. You know how they are. Ma ain't one for makin' mistakes if'n she can help it. She'll want it all worked out in her head before they make their move. So quit frettin'. You get on my nerves sometimes."

"Easy for you to say. You ain't sparkin' Cindy Lou like I am. I tell you, that gal is a temptress born and bred. She gets me so hot I can't think straight."

"That's my sister you're talkin' about, damn you. I don't hardly want to hear about you two frolickin' in clover."

"Do you reckon your ma will give her permission soon? It's been a whole year since I done asked. Surely that's long enough?"

"Ma makes up her mind in her own sweet time. Just don't pester her or she'll say no to spite you. She don't like being badgered. Even Pa treads soft around her. Believe you me, she can be a hellion when she's riled. I've got the scars on my back to prove it."

"I saw that time she tanned you with a cane. How you didn't let out a peep is beyond me."

"We daren't. If we cry out she hits us harder. She says a real man knows how to take punishment without flinchin'."

As the two men came around the outcropping, Nate strode onto the trail, his Hawken leveled. "I hope she taught you well." He thumbed back the hammer.

Both riders were taken off guard. They wore filthy homespun clothes and had on boots in desperate need of repair. Both sported beards, and their features were so alike they had to be related. The tall one on the right had rested his rifle across his thighs. The other rider didn't have a long gun.

They reined up, and the stocky one started to reach for a pistol.

"Go ahead. Try," Nate said. When the man froze, Nate took four paces backward. "Let your weapons fall. Do it real slow."

Neither of them obeyed. "What the hell is this all about?" the tall one demanded. "Who do you think you are, anyway?"

"I'm the man who is going to blow a hole in you the size of a melon if you don't do exactly as I say." Nate half hoped they would resist. They had tried to kill him; they had tried to kill his son. They deserved to have their wicks blown out.

The pair swapped glances. The tall one nodded. Gingerly, they dropped their guns and knives, one by one. As the short man let go of his knife, he said, "Listen, mister. We're just passin' through, is all. We don't mean anyone any harm. There's no call for you to be treatin' us like this unless you aim to rob us or some such."

"Climb off. Step in front of your horses."

"Like hell we will," the tall one growled.

Nate swiveled the Hawken's muzzle so it was squarely trained on the man's chest. "One way or the other, you're getting off. You choose."

"You son of a bitch," the tall one groused as he complied. "Here we are, mindin' our own business. We've never done nothin' to you. So what's this all about?"

The other one stared wistfully at the pistols he had dropped as he moved in front of his mare. "Now what?"

"Get down on your knees."

Wrath crackled on their brows as they did as they were bid. Glowering, the tall one balled his fists. "If'n you step close enough, I'm going to take that rifle and shove it so far up your ass, you'll have to shoot out your ears."

"Happy to oblige," Nate replied, and before they could react, he sprang in close and bashed the Hawken's heavy stock against the tall man's face. Cartilage crunched, scarlet spurted, and the man doubled over, clutching his face.

"My nose! My goddamn nose! You busted it!"

"I'm just getting started," Nate said. The short one tried to lunge upward, but Nate sidestepped and kicked him in the ribs. It pitched him onto his hands and knees. Not knowing when he was well off, the man shoved upward, only to be met midway by the Hawken's stock. This time it was an ear that crunched like a handful of dry twigs. Howling, the man fell, a hand pressed over the ruin.

Nate backed off. "Now that I've got your attention, you're going to answer some questions. We'll start with your names."

Some people truly never learned. "Go to hell!" roared the tall one. "We're not tellin' you a damn thing!"

"Care to bet?" Again Nate glided in close. Again the Hawken streaked down. The tall cutthroat thrust a hand out to ward off the blow, but all that did was allow his fingers to take the brunt. One snapped with a loud crack. Shrieking, the man came up off the ground in a rush. He was almost as big as Nate and almost as wide at the shoulders, but his reflexes were nowhere near as quick. The Hawken thundered, and a slug ripped through his thigh.

One of the horses bolted.

Nate instantly palmed a pistol. Sidling to the outcropping, he leaned the Hawken against it. The stocky stranger had sat up and was gawking at the tall one, who rolled back and forth in a paroxysm of torment. A crimson stain was spreading down his leg and drops of blood dripped from a hand he had clasped to the wound.

Nate pointed the pistol at the stocky one. "Your turn. What's your name?"

"Vin Coyfield."

"Your pard's?"

"Hap Coyfield."

"You're related."

"We're cousins." Raw hatred etched Vin's face. His ear was split wide, and his cheek and jaw were bright red.

"I heard mention of a mother and a sister. Where are they?"

Vin hesitated.

Nate was on him in a burst of speed, the pistol describing a tight arc that ended when it connected with the bridge of Vin's nose. Vin shrieked, then rallied and threw both arms around Nate's legs. But he did not grip them tight enough. Nate's knee caught him full in the mouth and Vin fell, arms waving feebly.

Hap Coyfield had stopped rolling and snorting and was glaring at the mountain man. "Mister, you'll suffer for this. God, how you'll suffer! Worse than the damned in the pit. My pa will skin you alive, chop you into tiny bits, and feed you to the scavengers. Just see if he don't!"

"Didn't this pa of yours ever teach you not to make threats when you're at the wrong end of a gun?" Nate saw Vin struggle to sit up. "You two have been spying on my family for close to a week. I want to know why."

"Eat dirt, you bastard. I'd rather be buzzard bait than tell you a thing."

"Suit yourself," Nate said, and shot Hap Coyfield through the head.

Vin recoiled, then whimpered and scrambled toward the outcropping as if to seek cover. "Sweet Jesus, sweet Jesus, sweet Jesus!"

Nate drew his second flintlock.

"Please, mister!" Vin pleaded while backing away. He scrambled up against the wall of rock and cringed in mortal fear of sharing his cousin's fate. "Don't kill me! For God's sake, please! I'll tell you anything you want to know! Honest!"

"Why were you spying on my family?"

"Our folks sent us. We were to keep an eye on you until we heard from 'em."

"You haven't answered my question. Why?"

Tears glistened as Vin nervously licked his lips. He looked at Hap's body. "Promise not to shoot me if I say?"

"So long as you tell me what I want to hear, you go on breathing."

"We're fixin' to settle in these parts. Cole, that's another cousin, he's taken a shine to your place. He wants it for his own. So him and that small Yankee woman can live by themselves. The rest of us will move into that cabin south of yours."

Only someone who knew Nate King well would have noticed how his jaw muscles twitched, how his eyes glinted like flint. "The Wards? Are they still alive?"

"Last I knew. We were to wait for word. No one's come yet, so I reckon they're fine."

"How many of you are there?"

Vin adopted a crafty look. "Only four. My pa, Hap's ma and pa, and Hap's sister, Cindy Lou."

"What about the other one you mentioned, Cole? That would make five."

Confusion rekindled Vin's fright. He began to count them off on his fingers, muttering to himself.

"It doesn't really matter." Nate extended the pistol. He would find out for himself soon enough.

"Wait! What are you doing?" Vin pressed flatter against the outcropping and pumped his hands. "You said I'd go on breathin' so long as I told you what you wanted to know! Don't your word count for anything?"

"I've learned all I need to."

"But you can't just up and kill a person in cold blood!" Vin's gaze drifted to Hap, and his Adam's apple bobbed. "All right. Maybe you can. But it ain't right. What did we ever do to you? Are you mad because we spied on your family? Because of the shot Hap took at you?''

''No. That's not why you have to die.''

''Then *what*?''

''You tried to kill my son.''

''I didn't really mean to! Honest! Please, just let me go and you'll never see me in these parts again!''

''You're a terrible liar.''

A bald eagle soaring high on the brisk currents above the regal peaks soared higher when the blast of a pistol rumbled upward like a peal of thunder.

Winona King had everything set to go. Parfleches crammed with food. Spare blankets. An extra pouch of ammunition for each of them. Whetstones, flint and steel. Even her husband's spyglass had been packed and placed on the table. So when the caw of a raven penetrated her sleep half an hour before sunrise, all she had to do was dress and fix breakfast while Nate saddled their horses and brought them to the front of the cabin. Little Evelyn tagged along to help him.

Zach and Louisa May Clark were also up, elbow to elbow next to the fire, whispering. Winona guessed what it was about. She pretended not to notice as she ran a brush through her long hair. A white man's brush, not the kind she had used as a girl, the one she still had, crafted from a porcupine's tail. Her grandmother had made it, sewing the tail over a long stick, then trimming the quills and stitching the seam with beadwork. It was so old, Winona was afraid it would fall apart.

The door opened and in came Nate. He had been uncharacteristically grim since he returned the night before, and Winona couldn't blame him. The Wards had become dear friends. If anything had happened to them— She shut the thought from her mind and finished her hair. ''I am ready when you are, husband.''

Zach and Lou stopped whispering as Nate walked toward them. They had been discussing whether they would be permitted to stay behind.

Zach slid his hands under his legs so no one would see him cross his fingers. "What will it be, Pa? Do you trust us enough?"

Nate had wrestled with the issue most of the night. Too worried about Simon and Felicity to fall sleep, he had tossed and turned until fatigue claimed him at four or so. "If a man can't trust his own son, who can he trust?"

Zach tried to think as his father would. "You figure there might be more of those fellas close by. You figure they'll come after us. But haven't I proven I can hold my own? I've outfought Blackfeet, the Sioux."

There was no denying that. But Nate had a much more crucial motive for the decision he had reached. "The two of you can stay. Someone has to look out for your sister. Your mother and I can't very well take her along now that we know for sure we're heading into trouble."

Evelyn overheard. A lively, lovely child, she was growing up to be the spitting image of her mother. And as outspoken. "I'm ten years old now, Pa. I can take care of myself."

"Of course you can," Nate said. But in reality, of course she *couldn't*. Against killers like the Coyfields she wouldn't stand a prayer. Children always wanted to be treated as adults, to be given the same privileges, the same freedoms. They tended to forget that those privileges and freedoms were earned through hard experience, the very experience that molded a boy or girl into a man or woman. "But you're to do as your brother says while we're gone. I don't want to hear you gave him any sass."

"Me?" Evelyn said innocently. Her brother and she were forever squabbling, snipping at each other like a cat and dog. It wasn't her fault Zach thought he knew it all and she knew he didn't.

Winona picked up two of the parfleches. She hid the apprehension that had resulted in a night almost as sleepless as her husband's. Like every mother, her innermost fear was of something terrible happening to her children. Most days the fear was buried deep, cloaked in the safety and normalcy of daily routine. But at times like this, when threats beyond her control confronted them, it roiled to the surface like scalding water in a geyser. And not all the composure she mustered could completely smother it.

Everyone filed outdoors. Nate stepped into the stirrups, then gazed south across the valley at a snow-crowned peak also visible from the Ward cabin. "We should be back in five days. If we not, head for Shakespeare's. Tell him to go see Touch the Clouds. A war party of Shoshones will set things right if we fail."

"You can count on me, Pa," Zach pledged.

Winona kissed her daughter and son and went to mount. Catching herself, she stepped to Louisa and kissed the girl on the cheek. "Take care of my son."

The last woman to kiss Lou had been her mother, ages before. For the first time since she had arrived at the Kings', Lou felt as if she were part of the family. A tingly feeling spread through her chest. Simultaneously, her throat became constricted as if she had a cold. "I will, Mrs. King. I'd give my life to save his."

Winona's mare was raring to go. She hadn't taken it for a ride in days. As she climbed on, it bobbed its head and took a few steps.

The mare's eagerness was contagious. "Let's go," Nate said, kneeing the stallion. "It'll take most of the day to get there as it is."

"Be careful, Pa!" Evelyn called out.

"Always. And you remember what I told you. Behave yourself."

Winona trailed her husband around the cabin. She shifted

to see her children one last time. Headstrong Zach, so intent on being acknowledged a man. Adorable Evelyn, so innocent, so vulnerable. And—yes—sweet Lou, who had known more grief in her sixteen years than most people knew in fifty. Winona smiled and waved and prayed she would see them again.

Chapter Seven

Felicity Ward wanted to scream. Or pick up a gun and shoot the Coyfields, one by one. She had never considered herself a violent person, but after the abuse she had suffered all afternoon she would gladly change. If not for her own sake, then for her husband's. Worry about Simon had further frayed her nerves. She was so overwrought, she kept glancing at the rifles propped near the door and gauging whether she could reach them before someone stopped her.

The Coyfields were animals. They had no regard for anyone or anything other than themselves.

Earlier, as soon as they hauled her back inside, Mabel demanded she set to work preparing more food. They were going to celebrate having a new place by having a midday meal fit for royalty. Felicity was constantly at the stove, cooking and roasting and baking, and fixing one pot of coffee after another.

At the same time, the Coyfields were tearing her home apart. They rooted into all the drawers, into the chest at the foot of the bed, into the cupboards, taking everything out, examining every article. Half the time they didn't bother putting anything back. They just dropped it on the floor. Clothes, blankets, towels now littered the cabin. Dishes were scattered on the counter. Pots and pans were everywhere. In a few short hours the clan had turned Felicity's clean and tidy haven into a pigsty.

When they weren't nosing around, the Coyfields were joking and laughing and thoroughly enjoying themselves. They hardly paid Felicity any mind except to bark for more coffee or more sweetcakes or more buttered biscuits.

The sole exception was Cole. He paid more attention to Felicity than she liked. Much more. His hungry eyes followed her everywhere. Lust shone on his swarthy face, and often, when she bent over, she caught him licking his lips in wicked relish. She loathed him. To her he was a hideous ogre, a disgusting lecher, the very worst humanity had to offer.

Once, when Felicity was carrying coffee to Jacob, Cole had put a hand on her. He'd reached out and placed a palm where only her husband had any right to place one. It startled her so, she dropped the cup and saucer. Adding shame to insult, he had brazenly started to fondle her, right there in front of the others.

Felicity had slapped his hand away and called him a pig. What did the rest of the Coyfields do? They laughed. Even the women. Even Mabel and Cindy Lou and Mary Beth. They all thought it was a great joke. Cole had reached for her again, but Mabel told him to quit it, that he should give Felicity time to get used to the idea.

Felicity almost burst into tears. The only thing that stopped her was the knowledge that they would only laugh harder, that her suffering was a source of amusement.

The Coyfields were unlike anyone Felicity had ever met. Even the slavers who stole her had not been as gleefully wicked, as blatantly vile. Now that there was no longer any need for them to put on their little act, they were showing their true natures, natures as dark as those of demons from the inferno. They were lustful, gluttonous savages.

It got worse once Bo Coyfield found the jug of whiskey under the counter. Simon had picked it up at a rendezvous and kept it around mainly to treat the mountain men who stopped by. Bo gave a whoop, and the next thing Felicity knew, all of them were helping themselves to greedy swigs. Before long the cabin reeked of liquor. What little self-control the Coyfields had evaporated, giving their wanton urges full rein.

Felicity saw things. She saw Tinder and Cindy Lou in a corner. That sparked an argument. Bo was upset at his brother because someone named Vin had "staked a claim" on Cindy Lou and it wasn't fair of Tinder to be trifling with her behind Vin's back. Tinder laughed and said what Vin didn't see wouldn't hurt him. Cindy Lou? She nuzzled Tinder's neck and ears the whole time, rubbing her lush body against his like a minx in heat.

The parents were little better. Jacob and Mabel were constantly touching each other where members of polite society touched only in private. Samuel, Felicity observed, gave Mabel certain looks on the sly, leading Felicity to wonder if Samuel and Mabel were more intimate than they should be. Maybe Jacob knew and didn't care.

Felicity wouldn't put anything past them. They were unspeakably foul. Yet to her amazement, they reveled in their depravity. They actually enjoyed being the way they were. She had heard of people like them. People who lacked a solitary shred of human decency. But she'd always imagined that the stories were exaggerated, that no one could be truly, completely evil. Now she knew better.

Unknown to Felicity, the worst shock was yet to come. Shortly before noon, Mabel turned to her and commented, "We'll be decidin' what to do with your husband pretty soon. Don't you do anything foolish and act up when the time comes."

Felicity didn't need to ask what "time" the woman referred to. "Can I see him? For just a minute?"

Jacob, who had overhead, lowered the jug, whiskey trickling over his lip. "What for? So's you can bawl and raise a fuss? I don't think so, gal."

"I won't act up. I promise." Felicity had never begged in her life, but she begged now. Clutching Mabel's thick fingers, she said, "Please. As a favor to me. Woman to woman. I only want to see if he's all right. I'll come right back in."

Mabel smiled and patted her arm. "All right, dearie. But you remember I did this for you. One favor deserves another." She looked up. "Cole, take her out to see her feller."

Felicity shook her head, blurting, "No. Not him. Not any of the men. I don't trust them as far as I can throw them." She saw the matriarch's eyes narrow and feared the insult would cost her the chance to see Simon. To her amazement, Mabel only chuckled.

"I don't blame you, little one. They're a horny bunch. Always wantin' to poke their baby-makers into us when we least expect. Were it up to me, I'd hack off all their members and spare us women a heap of aggravation."

Felicity couldn't help thinking, *This is a mother and a wife?* Aloud she asked, "Will you come along instead? I won't try anything."

"Oh, not me. I'm not as spry as I used to be." Mabel shifted and bellowed. "Mary Beth! Quit admirin' yourself in that mirror and get over here."

Samuel's daughter, who was in her early twenties, was the quietest of the clan. Mary Beth tended to keep to herself. Unlike her cousin, Cindy Lou, she showed no interest in any of the men. Felicity had pegged her as the best of the bunch, maybe someone she could persuade to help her if they were given a few moments alone. Now that wish was being fulfilled.

Hands clasped behind her shapely back, Mary Beth sashayed over. She wore a homespun dress a size too small, but it was cleaner than the clothes worn by the rest of her kin. Her full lips were always set in a perpetual pout, and she had a habit of stroking her long hair when she wasn't doing anything else. She also had a habit of never quite looking anyone in the eye when they spoke to her. "Yes, Aunt Mabel?"

"Take this gal out to see her gent."

Felicity took a step toward the door.

"Not so fast, dearie," Mabel said.

"What's wrong?"

Mabel pried the jug from her husband, savored a healthy swallow, then poked a thumb at Mary Beth. "She's got to check you first. Make sure you're not tryin' to sneak a knife or something out to him."

Felicity's own dress fit snugly from the waist up. She had removed her apron earlier. So, holding her arms out from her sides, she said, "Where would I hide anything?"

"Who can say?" Mabel said, smirking. "Once this woman stuck a razor up her sleeve. Another time, a man hid a folding knife in his britches. So I've learned not to leave anything to chance."

Mary Beth stepped in front of Felicity. "You heard my aunt."

"Go ahead, then," Felicity said, resigned. She figured it would be over quickly, that all Mary Beth had to do was pat her to verify she hadn't concealed a blade or other weapon on her person. Instead, Mary Beth probed everywhere. Under her arms, around her bosom, over her bosom. The whole while, Mary Beth grinned as if at some secret joke. Then Mary Beth bent down and Felicity felt fingers roving up under her dress. "Now, see here—!"

"You be still or you can forget seeing your man," Mabel warned. "Do you think that just because we're from the hills, we're stupid? It won't take but a minute."

It took longer. Much longer. Humiliation turned Felicity beet red. She had to clench her teeth and shut her eyes. When at long last Mary Beth straightened, Felicity took a deep breath and shuddered. She glared at the woman she had wrongly assumed to be the nicest of the Coyfields. Mary

David Thompson

Beth's face was flushed, too, and she was breathing heavily.

"Anything?" Mabel asked.

"Not so much as a sewin' needle."

"Get it done, then."

Simon Ward had not been idle. For hours he had been attempting to free himself. By constantly squirming and twisting, he was slowly but surely loosening the loops around his wrists. The effort cost him dearly, though. His skin was rubbed raw and his left wrist was bleeding profusely. But he refused to give up. Not while his beloved wife was in danger. Not while she was in there with those *fiends*.

The day was warm, a breeze fanning the grass. The rustling almost drowned out the sound of the cabin door opening and closing. Simon held himself still and rotated his arms so the blood on his wrists wouldn't be apparent. He figured it was one of the Coyfields, come to make sure he was still there.

The sight of Felicity stirred Simon to the depths of his soul. Maybe it was the sunlight bathing her hair and face, or maybe it was the relief that washed over him, but her beauty had never moved him as deeply as it did at this moment. The worry in her eyes stirred him, too, and for her sake he forced a smile. "Thank God they haven't harmed you!"

Felicity was too choked with emotion to talk. She knelt, tenderly resting a hand on his cheek. Tears fought for release, and she struggled to contain them.

"How are you holding up?" Simon asked.

Just awful, Felicity was inclined to say. But what came out was "I'm doing fine. They leave me pretty much alone. Mabel let me come out to see you. Maybe she'll also let me bring you some water and food."

Mary Beth tittered. "Forget it, city gal. He's fine as he is. He won't be needin' nourishment before too long, anyhow."

Despite Felicity's desire, a single tear seeped from the corner of her right eye and trickled down her cheek. "I'm sorry, Simon. I'm so, so sorry."

"For what?"

"For being a fool. For being too trusting. For taking it for granted these people would be nice just because we are."

His wife's turmoil filled Simon with the same. He yearned to take her in his arms, to comfort her, to assure her she wasn't to blame for the darkness that ruled the hearts of others. "Things will work out just fine. Wait and see."

Mary Beth Coyfield cackled. "I thought my cousin Hap was dumb, but mister, you've got him beat all hollow. Did a horse stomp on you when you were a kid and damage your think box?"

Felicity grasped Simon's shirt, in need of something to anchor her, afraid she would jump up and do something she would regret. "Can't you let us be for a minute, damn you!"

"Now, now," Mary Beth replied. "Keep a civil tongue or you go right back inside. Mabel said I was to bring you out. She didn't say how long I had to let you stay."

Swallowing her pride, Felicity said, "I'm sorry. It's the strain. I would be grateful if you would let me have a few words with my husband alone."

"I can't hardly allow that. But I will move back a ways so's you can make cow eyes at one another and whisper your farewells." Chuckling, Mary Beth retreated ten feet or so.

Felicity bent low, her lips nearly brushing Simon's. "I hate her. I hate all of them. If I could get my hands on a gun—!"

The vehemence in his wife's tone stunned Simon. She had always been the gentlest of people, as kind as the year was long. Always ready to lend a helping hand. To give others the benefit of the doubt. "Don't try. They'll kill you."

"And what do you think they're going to do to you?" Felicity said more sharply than she meant to. "I have to do something. You heard that tart. You don't have much time.

And I won't let them hurt you, even if it costs me my own life. You're everything to me, Simon.''

Under more pleasant circumstances, her declaration would have inspired Simon to embrace her and smother her with kisses. Now he said, "Please, listen to me. Don't do a thing to provoke them. I couldn't bear it if they harmed you.''

"I won't let them kill you," Felicity stressed. On an impulse, she glued her lips to his, giving him the kind of kiss that always took his breath away, the kind that set her heart to fluttering. She didn't care that Mary Beth was watching. When she broke for air, she whispered, "Listen closely. I'm going to start back. When I get to the flower garden, I'm going to say my shoe needs lacing. But what I'm really going to do is take that big rock at the corner of the garden and hit the tart over the head. If I can knock her out, I'll free you and we'll escape.''

"No. It's too dangerous.''

"Darling, it's the only chance we have.''

Simon couldn't argue with the truth, but he refused to let her put herself in jeopardy. He went to say as much when he saw Mary Beth Coyfield materialize over her shoulder.

"Time's up, city gal.''

Felicity kissed Simon on the tip of his nose, smiled, and slowly rose. All the love in her being poured from her eyes, and the love that streamed from his gave her added incentive to do what she must. Turning, she headed back, her head bowed to give the impression she was too stricken with grief to cause any trouble.

Halfway there Mary Beth's hand closed on her wrist. "Hold up.''

"What?''

"How about you and me go for a stroll? Say, over yonder by those trees. Ma will understand. And if'n you let me, I'll fetch some water for your man after we're done. What do you say?''

"Let you what?" Felicity said, not comprehending until the lusty gleam in the other's eyes gave her a clue. The suggestion so revolted her that she raised a hand to slap Mary Beth's face. Only the thought that it would spoil her plan to save Simon stopped her.

"So I take it the answer is no, Miss High-and-Mighty?"

Felicity knew a spot, a quiet glade where downed limbs were handy. What if she led Mary Beth there? What if she got Mary Beth to turn her back, then hit her with one of the limbs? It would be safer than at the flower garden. "I might be interested," she said, but Fate denied her the opportunity.

Mary Beth was gazing toward the cabin. "Damnation. Looks like we can forget it. I never get to have any fun."

Mabel, Cole, Jess, and Bo had come out. Mabel beckoned, saying, "Time's up, dearie. Mary Beth, you get inside and help your sister set the table."

"Why can't this Yankee do it?" Mary Beth said. "You know how I hate housework."

"And you know how I hate to be sassed. Get that contrary backside of yours in there before I have Cole find me a switch. I need to have a talk with the little missy."

Sighing, Mary Beth brushed a hand across Felicity's arm. "Your loss. I'd have had you floating in the clouds." Pouting, she flounced off.

Felicity followed. It was difficult to hide her disappointment at being thwarted. Now she had no hope of freeing Simon. She glanced back but couldn't see him for the high grass. *I will find a way, my beloved!* she promised.

Bo and Jess had their rifles. Over their shoulders were pouches crammed with jerked buffalo meat, meat that belonged to the Wards.

"I reckon we're all set, Ma," Jess said.

Mabel put her hands on her broad hips and thoughtfully regarded the youngest members of the clan. "We're countin' on you two. Don't let us down. Hook up with Hap and Vin and rub out this King feller.'' She paused. ''He might be on his way here. If'n you seé him comin', hide and let him pass you by. Don't try and make wolf meat of him on your own. Hear me?''

''What do you want done with the 'breeds and the white girl?'' Jess asked.

''Don't touch the white girl. As for the halfbreeds, if'n you don't know what to do with them, you're stupider than snot. Though maybe the 'breed girl is worth keepin', if'n one of you cottons to her. Just keep in mind it'll be a couple of years yet before she's ripe for pokin'.''

Felicity knew they were talking about Evelyn; her disgust reached new heights. ''That girl is only ten. She's a child.''

''So?'' Mabel replied. ''My brother diddled me for the first time when I was eleven. Didn't do me no harm. I reckon I'm doing this girl a favor by havin' my boys wait until she's twelve.'' Turning back to Jess and Bo, she said, ''Your pas and me are countin' on you. This is the first time we've let you do something like this without us there to make sure you don't make mistakes. Remember all the things we've taught you. Listen to Hap and Vin. They've kilt plenty of jaspers and know just how to go about it.''

Jess hefted his Kentucky. ''We'll be fine, Ma. Quit treatin' us like we haven't been weaned. Remember who it was shot that farmer in Arkansas?''

''And you remember that what I told Mary Beth applies to you. I won't take no sass.'' Mabel grinned at Samuel's son. ''Bo, you've always had enough horse sense to spare. Keep an eye on Jess. Sometimes he lets his hankerin's get the better of him.''

''You can count on me, Aunt Mabel.''

Cole Coyfield wasn't looking at either of them. He had eyes only for Felicity. She ignored him, even when he came closer and leered at her as if she were a streetwalker.

The two youngest walked to their mules and mounted.

Mabel waved as they rode off, remarking, "It does a mother's heart proud to have a son and a nephew like those two. The Lord knows I have some flaws, but I've done a good job of raisin' my brood, if'n I do say so myself."

"You can't be serious," Felicity said, and never saw the hand that struck her. Rocked on her heels, she had to bear the added sting of Cole's coarse laughter.

"When you have kids of your own, then you can criticize," Mabel said indignantly. "I've done the best I could with the talents I was given. Maybe by your highfalutin standards that's not good enough. But none of my boys are drunkards. Or wastin' away in prison. They've done me proud."

Felicity couldn't believe what she was hearing. The woman had raised a pack of cold-blooded murderers, yet had the gall to brag because none of them were behind bars? "By their fruits ye shall know them."

"What's that supposed to mean?" Cole demanded.

Mabel snorted. "She's sayin' we're swine, son. She thinks we're so ignorant, we ain't ever read Scripture. Frankly, boy, I'm commencin' to think she's more bother than she's worth. She'll make you a miserable wife. Always gripin' and lookin' down that little nose of hers at us."

"Not if I slap her around, she won't." Cole appeared ready to do it then and there.

"Go on in," Mabel said. "Me and her need to have a woman-to-woman chat."

"About what?" Felicity inquired when the lecher was gone.

"About you, missy. About your attitude. Did you think I wouldn't notice how you've been actin' all day? I've met your kind before. You believe you're too good for everyone else. That the Almighty made you perfect and the rest of us ain't but miserable sinners." She raised a hand when Felicity tried to respond. "I ain't done. Cole has his sights set on you, and I ain't about to deny him. He's the oldest, my first, and they're always special. But were it up to me, I'd have you gutted and tossed into the same hole as your man.''

"I wish you would kill me too," Felicity said, and she meant it. She would rather die than go on living without Simon.

"Weren't you listenin'? You're going to be Cole's wife whether you like the notion or not. So we need to talk about whether we do this the easy way or the hard.''

"There *is* an easy way?" Felicity quipped. In her opinion, nothing could make so hideous an outcome bearable.

"That's up to you. You can raise a stink. You can bitch and moan. You can treat my Cole like dirt and lay there like a lump when he's feelin' frisky. But then all you'll get is grief and more grief. I can be mean when I want to.''

What do you call how you have been? Felicity inwardly shouted. Rather than provoke another cuffing, she asked, "What's your point?"

"I want you to treat Cole decent. I want you to be the best wife you can be.''

Felicity could only stare.

"A favor for a favor, missy. I did you one by lettin' you go to your hubby. Now you can do me one by makin' Cole happy.''

"Never.''

"It might be in your best interest to reconsider. Whether a person is fed to the gators one piece at a time or tossed in whole don't make much of a difference except to the person the gators eat.''

Felicity wasn't quite sure she understood, and said so.

"Let me make it plain, then. Your man can die quick or he can die slow. Quick, we put a bullet in his head and there's little pain. Slow, I have one of my menfolk whittle on him like he's a piece of wood. We'd start by chopping off his fingers and toes. Then we'd chop off other parts, if'n you get my drift.''

"Surely you wouldn't!"

"Please, dearie. You must know me better than that by now. I'm a woman of my word. Either you agree to do as I want or your husband will die a death I wouldn't wish on an Injun. You'll hear his screams the rest of your days. And you'll never shake the memory of how he looks with stumps for arms and no manhood to speak of.''

Total, utter loathing filled Felicity. "You'd make me watch?''

"To punish you. It's what you deserve if you turn me down." Mabel's features grew as rigid as marble. "So what will it be? Will you take up with Cole without any fuss? Or will you be pigheaded and make your husband suffer?''

It was no choice at all. Felicity bowed her head again, this time in real grief. She would rather be torn limb from limb by ravening beasts than let Cole Coyfield put his foul hands on her. But she would do anything to spare Simon more misery. Even if that meant the unthinkable.

"I want your decision," Mabel pressed her.

"If I agree, will you let me see Simon one more time?''

Mabel knew she had won. Smiling in triumph, she placed a hand on one of her pistols. "Hell, we'll go visit him right this second if it will make you feel better. Then I'll spring the good news on Cole.''

Felicity glumly dogged the heavyset woman's heels. She thought of grabbing a rock, of doing as she had planned to do with Mary Beth. But Mabel was five times her size and as strong as a man. Trying to bring her down would be like trying to bring down a tough old boar. Lost in sorrow, Felicity didn't realize Mabel had stopped until she bumped into Mabel's back.

"Son of a bitch!"

Felicity stepped to the left so she could see her husband.

In a heartbeat she was hurled from the depths of despair to the heights of joy. Elation coursed through her, and she wanted to shout for joy.

Simon was gone!

Chapter Eight

It was the idea of his wife about to do something that could get her killed that spurred Simon Ward into escaping. He had been trying for hours without success. On seeing how distraught she had become, he realized he must break free quickly, before she brought the Coyfields' wrath down on her head.

So, clenching his teeth against the agony, Simon twisted and turned his forearms without letup. Soon both were slick with blood, but he didn't stop. The blood helped. It made his wrists slippery enough that with a lot of effort and a dollop of luck, he might finally be able to slide his hands from the loops.

Simon heard the Coyfields talking in front of the cabin. The comment about killing Nate King filled him with horror, lending added incentive. He couldn't let anything happen to the Kings. They were wonderful, sweet people. The salt of the earth. Even moody Zach had proven himself a friend. So now, in addition to saving his wife, Simon must somehow save his neighbors.

Thudding hoofs galvanized Simon into throwing his whole body into the attempt. The strain on his shoulders and hips was incredible. But he went on thrashing and churning until the pain threatened to make him black out. Sagging, exhausted, caked with sweat, he resisted a flood tide of bitter disappointment. It was hopeless. He couldn't get loose even though his life depended on it!

Angry at his failure, Simon jerked on his right arm in frustration. Suddenly, right in front of his eyes, was his hand. The wrist had been torn raw, the flesh was seared deep. Blood caked the sleeve. But he was free! Swiftly, Simon turned his full attention to his left wrist. Prying at the knots, he soon loosened them enough to free his other arm.

Simon made short shrift of the loops binding his ankles. No one had appeared. He thought of rushing to his wife's side, but he'd heard Cole's voice a short while before. Unarmed, Simon would be no match for the hulking bruiser.

Reluctantly, Simon dashed into the high grass and circled around behind the cabin. When he was abreast of the corral, he halted. He had a decision to make. Should he stay and help Felicity? Or should he steal a mount and fly to Nate's for help? Such a heartrending choice! It would take all day and most of the night to reach the King cabin. By then, who knew what the Coyfields would do to Felicity?

The matter was taken out of Simon's hands by a throaty bellow to the south.

"Jacob! Samuel! Get everyone out here! He's gone! The damned Yankee has busted loose!"

Simon couldn't hope to open the gate, throw a bridle on a horse, and ride off before the Coyfields spotted him. So he spun and ran, staying bent low. He had to find somewhere to hide, somewhere to lie low until nightfall. Since he knew the valley better than his enemies, he stood a good chance of eluding them.

On second thought, Simon had doubts. They were hill folk. Which meant they were probably skilled hunters, skilled trackers. Like a pack of bloodhounds, they would trail him to the ends of the earth.

There was one small consolation. With the two youngest, Jess and Bo, gone, his prospects were slightly better. Now there were only four men and three women left. *Only!* Seven against one were hardly fair odds. Seven against two, he corrected himself. He mustn't forget Felicity.

Simon was fifty yards from the cabin when Jacob's voice thundered.

"Spread out! Find his tracks! I want him alive! Wound him if need be! But I want the son of a bitch!"

With wings on his feet, Simon angled to the southeast, toward the nearest woodland. His wrists were aflame and his shoulders throbbed, but he shut the distress from his mind. He covered another twenty yards. Then Cole Coyfield gave a whoop.

"Here, Pa! Over here are his tracks! He's makin' off through the grass!"

Simon straightened and ran. He had hardly taken two steps before a rifle cracked and a slug nearly took off his right ear.

"No shootin', Tinder, you cussed idiot!" Jacob bawled. "We want him breathin' yet, remember?"

It made no sense to Simon. They wanted him alive just so they could murder him later? He sprinted on, running as he had never run before, the grass swishing against his legs. A glance showed that Cole, Tinder, and—of all people—Mary Beth had given chase. Tinder was far back, but Mary Beth and Cole were coming on fast, with Cole slightly in the lead.

Simon spied Felicity by the cabin, ringed by Jacob, Mabel, and Samuel. He smiled to encourage her but couldn't tell if she noticed or responded. Of Cindy Lou there was no trace.

Legs pumping, Simon concentrated on the tree line. The undergrowth would be his salvation. It would slow him down, but it would also slow down the Coyfields. And if he remembered what Nate King had taught him, if he stuck to the hardest ground and was careful about leaving tracks, he could elude them. That was his plan, anyway.

The nicker of a horse alerted him to a potential hitch. The reason Simon had not spotted Cindy Lou was that she had been at the corral, saddling a pair of mounts. Now, astride one and leading the other, she galloped after her kin.

The distance between Simon and the trees was less than that between him and Cindy Lou. But a horse could cover ground five times as swiftly as a man. She might overtake him before he reached cover.

"Go, gal! Go!" Mabel hollered.

Felicity Ward had her hands pressed to her throat. In wide-eyed fear, she watched her beloved's race for life and wished she were at his side. Barring that, she wished she might lend him speed and stamina.

Cindy Lou had passed Tinder and almost caught up with Mary Beth, who was amazingly fleet of foot. Mary Beth slowed, holding out a hand for the reins of the spare horse. But Cindy Lou sped past her, onward a dozen feet to Cole.

"Brother! Here!"

Cole Coyfield took one look, pivoted in midstride, and was ready when the spare mount came even with him. Snagging the saddle, he swung up, seized the reins, and smacked his legs against the gelding's sides. Cindy Lou had shot on by, but he swiftly caught up. They were now less than thirty yards behind Simon.

Forgetting herself, Felicity shouted, "Run, Simon! In heaven's name, run!"

Mabel whipped around and backhanded Felicity across the mouth. "Hush, damn you! You'd best hope we catch that man of yours quick. The harder he makes it on us, the harder we'll make it on him."

Holding her bloody mouth, Felicity felt intense fury roil in her like boiling lava in a volcano. She wanted to strike out, to hit Mabel in the face again and again, to go on hitting until Mabel was unconscious, or dead. Felicity didn't care which. She wanted the mother and all the Coyfields dead. *Dead, dead, dead!* And she didn't feel the least bit guilty. Felicity had never thought she would want to slay anyone, but if there was ever anyone who *deserved* to be slain, it was the Coyfields.

Samuel was yelling for his boy Tinder to run faster, to catch up with the others. In his excitement he failed to realize one of his pistols was within easy reach.

Felicity glanced at Jacob and Mabel. The former was glued to the chase. The latter was urging Cole and Cindy Lou to ride like the wind. Lunging, Felicity grabbed the butt of Samuel's flintlock. She had it out and was cocking it when Samuel spun toward her. "Don't move! None of you!" Felicity backpedaled, swinging the muzzle from one Coyfield to the other.

Jacob sneered, then growled at his brother, "What do you use for brains? Mush? How could you let her make a jackass of you?"

Mabel wasn't the least bit worried. "It's your gun, Sam. Take it from her."

Felicity was trying to keep on eye on them and one on Simon. He was close to cover, but Cole and Cindy Lou were close to him. "I want all of you to drop your weapons, or else."

"Or else what, dearie?" Mabel retorted. "You can only shoot one of us. And as soon as you do, the other two of us will beat you into the ground."

"Which one of you is eager to die, then?" Felicity challenged, aiming at Mabel. "How about you, you despicable woman? Or maybe your pig of a husband?" Felicity pointed the pistol at Jacob.

"I don't take kindly to being called names," Jacob said.

"Who cares?" Felicity practically screeched. She was so agitated, her whole body shook. With every fiber of her being she *wanted* to squeeze that trigger.

Mabel's fleshy chin lifted in an oily smile. "Calm down, Yank. You're liable to have a conniption." She took a half-step. "Maybe I was a mite hasty. Put down that gun and I

107

give you my word that we'll go easy on you."

"You lying witch! I wouldn't believe you if you swore on a stack of Bibles. You're scum, the whole bunch of you!" Again Felicity checked on her husband. Simon was almost to the forest. But Cole had raised his rifle and was taking deliberate aim. "Simon!" she shouted. "Look out!"

At that very instant, when she was distracted, all three of the Coyfields rushed her. Samuel was nearest. Felicity fired, the flash of the pan followed by the blast of the smoothbore. Samuel wrenched sideways but was still struck. Knocked backward, he staggered. Felicity sought to flee, but Jacob was on her with a quickness his bulk belied. A callused hand seized her right wrist. She punched at his neck, at his chin, but it was like striking a pillow. The rolls and folds of fat absorbed her blows. He barely felt them.

"Let go!" Felicity said, struggling her utmost. She would have been better off saving her breath, for the next second Mabel drove a fist into her stomach. It was like being kicked by a mule. All the air in Felicity's lungs whooshed between her parted lips and she doubled over.

"Yankee bitch!" Mabel raged, raining fists. "You shot my Sam! I'll bust every bone in your body!"

Felicity shriveled like a flower under a deluge of hailstones. Tucking her chin to her chest, she tried to ward off the onslaught, but it was impossible. Her head, her shoulders, were brutally boxed and clubbed. She attempted to scramble away, but Jacob held on to her arm. An ear, her cheek, an eyebrow were savagely pummeled. The butt of a pistol slammed into her next. Her head swam and she was on the verge of passing out when a gun cracked in the distance.

The beating ceased.

"Did you see, Ma? He got the varmint!" Jacob exclaimed. "Cole shot the Yankee!"

An inky veil claimed Felicity.

*   *   *

Simon Ward was only a few feet from the pines when the rifle discharged. Something seemed to push against his back, low down on the left side. Propelled forward like a child's doll, he stumbled and would have fallen if not for a small pine he snared and held on to. Lancing pains racked him.

The jagged exit wound poured blood. Simon clamped a palm over it and ran on. He barreled into the thicket, paying no mind to the many sharp branches that tore at his clothes.

The drumming of hooves was much too close. Simon flattened and crawled, scuttling like an oversized crab. Slanting to the left, to the north, he snaked among the prickly plants, thankful they pressed in so close above.

Horses arrived at the undergrowth's edge. "Where'd he go?" Cole said irritably. "I lost track of him!"

"He can't have gotten far," Cindy Lou responded. "You go right, I'll go left. As soon as you find his tracks, give a holler."

Simon froze. He saw the legs of Cindy's mount bearing wide to one side. Cole's horse he could only hear. He braced for an outcry. They were bound to spot him. But Cindy's animal trotted within seven or eight feet of where he lay and she never said a word. The only explanation he could think of was that she must be scouring the woods up ahead. They must have believed he had gone on *through* the thicket.

"I still don't see him!" Cole complained.

"Keep looking! He can't have gotten far!"

Brush crackled to the passage of their mounts. Simon listened to the noise dwindle. He was set to rise when footsteps pattered. Out of the corner of an eye he caught fleeting sight of Mary Lou. She had a long knife in her right hand. Pausing, she looked right and left, then ran after her cousins.

After mentally counting to ten, Simon rose onto his hands and knees and heaved out of the thicket. His cheek was cut, his temple gouged. He saw Mary Lou's retreating figure, grinned, and started to run to the north.

Around a tree came Tinder Coyfield. It was difficult to say which of them was more surprised. Tinder snapped up his Kentucky and jerked back the hammer. Simon leaped, but he had two yards to cover and the hammer descended before he could make it. Instead of a flash of flame and smoke, though, there was a dry click. Tinder had neglected to reload after firing earlier.

Simon reached the burly backwoodsman as Tinder made a play for a pistol. Gripping the Kentucky, Simon ripped it from the southerner's grasp. As Tinder flourished the pistol, Simon swung the rifle like an ax. It slammed into Tinder's jaw. Tinder was jarred backward and collided with the trunk of a tree behind him. Simon drew back the rifle a second time. Tinder's pistol was centering on his chest when the stock connected with the side of Tinder's head. Samuel's son collapsed like a house of cards.

Simon didn't waste another precious moment. Squatting, he removed Tinder's ammo pouch and powder horn and slung them across his own chest. Tinder's pistols went under his belt. In his hurry to get away before one of the others returned, Simon ran off without taking Tinder's knife. He had no plan, other than to elude the Coyfields. Once he had, he would ponder how to save Felicity.

Simon prayed she was all right.

A sensation of wetness revived her. Felicity blinked and coughed as water got into her mouth and nose. She sat up, sputtering, and found she was in the cabin by the crackling fire. For several seconds she was disoriented. She couldn't recall how she had gotten there or what had happened to her last. Vaguely, she recalled Simon being in peril.

"Up and at 'em, Yankee. We want some supper."

Felicity saw Mabel Coyfield standing over her, holding an upended glass. The memory of their clash pierced her like a sword. "Simon!" she cried, pushing to her feet. "Where is he? What have you done to him?"

"Not what I'd like to do, that's for sure," Mabel said. At the table were Jacob and Samuel, sharing the jug. Tinder was in the rocking chair, being doctored by Cindy Lou. Cole hunkered in a corner, cleaning his rifle.

"He escaped?" Felicity said. The matriarch need not answer. Mabel's expression was answer enough. A thrill rippled through Felicity, and she grinned. "He escaped!"

"Only for a while, missy. Soon as it's daylight we're fixin' to hunt him down." Mabel walked toward the table.

"And we've got the perfect bait," Jacob said, winking at his wife.

Felicity didn't like the sound of that.

" 'Course, we might not have to go to any bother," Cole said with a wicked leer. "Not if my she-cat of a cousin finds him first."

Not until that moment did Felicity realize one of the clan was missing. "Where's Mary Beth?"

"Where do you think?" Cole rejoined. "Once she gets on a scent she won't let up. She's part wildcat, part wolverine. Once, down to Arkansas, she went after two men who tried to bushwhack Ma and Pa. Tracked 'em for days, she did. Came up on the pair when they were sleepin' and slit their throats as pretty as you please."

Samuel chuckled. His shirt was off and his side had been crudely bandaged. Evidently, the gunshot had not been severe. "That's my gal. She can lick her weight in fellas any day of the week. Mary Beth never has liked menfolk much, but I reckon you know that already, don't you, city lady?"

The idea of Simon, alone in the wilderness and being stalked by the man-hater, scared Felicity worse than if he were being stalked by a grizzly. "I remember hearing one of you say my husband had been shot."

Cole was sliding the ramrod into his rifle. "I thought I hit him, but now I don't know. We never found any blood.''

Mabel gestured at the stove. "Enough jawin'. It's the shank of the evening. Fix us some vittles, missy. A stew would be nice. Pa shot a rabbit before the light faded. It's on the counter.''

Felicity was almost glad for something to do. It gave her time to think. The despair that had afflicted her was gone thanks to Simon being on the loose. Now anything was possible. The two of them together could beat any foe.

Tinder stood. His jaw was swollen and discolored and he had a nasty gash on his head. Gingerly touching his puffy lower lip, he said, "I hope to hell Mary Beth brings the Yankee back alive. I owe him."

Samuel showed no sympathy for his son. "That's what you get for being sloppy, boy. How many times do I have to tell you? As soon as you shoot, reload. One of these days you'll be caught with an empty gun and it'll cost you your life."

Cindy Lou slid into the rocker and placed her feet on the stones flanking the fireplace. "If'n it was me, Cousin Tinder, I wouldn't count on makin' that feller pay. Mary Beth will likely carve him into little bits and pieces." Cindy Lou smirked at Felicity. "Wouldn't surprise me none if she chops off your feller's manhood and makes him eat it."

"You're pure and utter filth," Felicity said.

"Sticks and stones, Yankee. I'm only tellin' you how it is." Cindy Lou stretched languidly, like a cat about to lick itself. "It's a shame, too. I thought your husband was kind of cute."

"He'd never soil himself with a harpy like you."

Mabel had taken a seat and helped herself to the jug. "Watch that mouth of yours. Get my dander up and you'll regret it." Swallowing, she smacked her lips. "Seems to me you ought to be thankin' my boy. The only reason you're not breathin' dirt is because Cole has taken a fancy to you.

Although, for the life of me, I'm beginnin' to question what he sees in such a scrawny snippet."

"Ah, Ma," Cole said. "She is a mite puny, but you said yourself that she's a peach. And she has a heap of spunk. Look at how she stood up to you."

"Spunk is one thing. No brains is another."

They prattled on about women Cole had known back in the States, comparing them to Felicity, but Felicity wasn't listening. Simon occupied her thoughts. Where was he? What was he doing? She tried to put herself in his boots and guess when he would make a bid to free her. Because as surely as she lived and breathed, he would try.

Opening a drawer, Felicity selected a knife so she could prepare the rabbit. None of the Coyfields showed any alarm at her being armed. But Jacob did draw a pistol and lay it on the table.

As Felicity sank the steel into the rabbit's belly, she envisioned it being Mabel's. As she sliced from front to back, she imagined doing the same to each of the clan. When she cut into the guts, she was cutting into Jacob. When she hacked at the intestines, she was hacking at Samuel. And when she lopped off the rabbit's head, it was Cindy Lou's head that rolled onto the floor.

Felicity grinned. Skinning a rabbit had never been so much fun.

Simon Ward halted to take his bearings. By his best reckoning he was northwest of the cabin. A mile, perhaps a little more. Ever since darkness claimed the Rockies his senses of direction and distance were as poor as a rock's. Not that it was anything to brag about during the day. As Shakespeare McNair once joked, if it weren't for the sun, Simon wouldn't know east from west.

Mountain men like McNair and Nate King possessed an uncanny knack in that regard. They always knew where they were in relation to everything else, almost as if they were born gifted with internal compasses. Simon had seen Nate navigate rugged slopes in dense fog as unerringly as if it were a sunny day. He was with Nate one time when they were caught high up on Longs Peak by an early snowstorm. Had Simon been alone, he'd never have made it down alive. Yet Nate guided them through snow so heavy, Simon couldn't see his fingers at arm's length.

Now Simon scanned the heavens for the North Star. Nate had taught him how to find it. All he had to do was locate the Big Dipper. The two stars that formed the side of the dipper away from the handle pointed to another bright star all by itself. This was the North Star, so named because it was always directly above the North Pole.

Finding it, Simon verified he was where he thought he was. From the ridge on which he stood, a square of light marked hearth and home. He longed to rush there, to tear his wife from the clutches of those devils in human guise. But he must be patient. For her sake, as well as his.

A convenient boulder offered Simon a roost. Wearily, he sat and leaned on the Kentucky. His side ached worse than a decayed tooth. It needed tending, but the best he had been able to do was splash water on it. Probing with a forefinger earlier revealed the ball had penetrated the soft flesh below his ribs and ruptured out above his hipbone. That it hadn't struck a vital organ was a miracle. That he hadn't bled to death was another.

Simon had lost a lot of blood. Much too much. He'd attempted to stem the flow, first with grass, then with leaves, then with mud from the bank of the stream. Only the mud worked. But he was concerned lest infection set in. According to Nate, more men died from lead poisoning and other complications than from the bullet itself.

Simon's eyelids were heavy, his limbs felt as if they weighed a ton. Fatigue gnawed at him, but he shook it off.

Felicity was uppermost on his mind. He had to sneak down there, had to spirit her away. But *how*? What chance did he have alone? Simon wasn't about to kid himself. His escape had been more a product of luck than cunning.

A rustling noise brought Simon's head up. He had heard the same sound off and on throughout the day. When he was on the valley floor he had attributed it to wind rustling the grass. But once he was higher up, where grass was sparse, he'd still heard it. For a while he had just figured it was the breeze shaking leaves.

Over the course of the past hour, however, Simon had been plagued by a persistent feeling that he was being followed. He'd gone into cover several times to wait and see if anyone came along, but no one ever did. So now he blamed his overwrought nerves.

Simon started to rise, then thought better of it. Why tire himself more? Sliding off the boulder, he leaned against it and cradled the Kentucky in his lap. Lord, he was spent. He could sleep for a week. But he dared not doze off. In the middle of the night he had to make his way back down. By then the Coyfields were bound to be asleep. He would burst in among them and spirit Felicity out of there. He couldn't wait.

Simon's eyes closed of their own accord. He told himself it would only be for a few minutes. That he wouldn't drift off. Yet when he opened his eyes next, the positions of the stars had changed slightly. Enough to indicate he had slept half an hour, maybe more. Grunting, he rose up onto the boulder again, where he was less comfortable and less likely to succumb.

Simon could never say what made him look over his shoulder. He had not heard anything. He had not sensed anything. But he looked, and was startled to behold a shadowy figure almost on top of him, as if it had been creeping toward

115

him and stopped when he unexpectedly changed position. "Who the—?" he blurted.

With that, the figure screeched like a banshee and flung itself at him.

Chapter Nine

About the same time Simon Ward had been making his escape, much farther north Nate and Winona King were goading their mounts up a steep switchback toward the pass that linked the two valleys. They had held to a brisk pace all day. Horses and riders alike were tired, but Nate refused to rest, even briefly. Not when every minute counted.

Nate valued friendship as much as he valued family. To his way of thinking, good friends, truly close friends, *were* family. More than a dozen Shoshone warriors had earned his undying trust, while the number of white friends he had could be counted on one hand. Not that he wouldn't like more. It was just that so few whites lived in the Rockies. Shakespeare McNair, Scott Kendall, and Simon Ward were the nearest and dearest. There wasn't a blessed thing Nate wouldn't do for them or they for him.

The type of lives they lived was partly responsible. Hardship forged bonds of steel. When two people had to rely on each other or perish, they came closer together than they ever would otherwise. Necessity forced them to open up, to break down the walls that too often kept people from cementing ties of genuine friendship.

Back in the States it was different. There, a person could pretend to be someone's friend, all the while talking about them behind their back. There, a person could claim to be a friend, but when they were needed, when the friendship was put to the test, they always had an excuse as to why they couldn't lend a hand. The proof of the pudding was in the tasting, as the saying went, and too many failed the test.

A true friend was always there when he had to be. A true friend would give the shirt off his back, the last dollar in his pocket. A true friend listened without judging, shared without expecting anything in return. A true friend was like gold, making even paupers rich.

Since these were Nate's innermost sentiments, it's no wonder he was so anxious to reach the Ward cabin. All day he had been chafing at what he considered their snail's pace. All day he had been going over in his head the route they must take and thinking of ways they might shave hours off the journey.

Now, as they came to the top of the switchback, Nate reined up and gazed at a gap in a stark cliff high above. "The pass," he said aloud.

Winona nodded. She shared her husband's apprehension. Although Felicity Ward and she came from vastly different cultures, they had grown remarkably close. Felicity had shown Winona it was possible for white and red women to care for one another as sisters. That not all whites looked down their noses at Indians.

To be fair, Winona had made other white friends. But few were as cherished as Felicity. The many hours they had spent together, sharing tales of the many silly things their husbands did, had shown them how much they had in common. And in that common soil the seeds of friendship took root and thrived.

"Care for a drink, husband?" Winona asked, twisting to place a hand on the water skin tied to her saddle.

"Why not?" Nate said. It was the first they had treated themselves to since they rode out that morning. Swinging down, he accepted the skin and tilted it to his mouth.

Winona watched his throat as he drank, thinking of how she had nibbled on that spot the night before when they were cuddling in bed. It amazed her sometimes, how after all these years she still loved this man so much. How he still kindled passions no other ever could. How he had become everything to her, and she to him.

Nate finished and handed the water skin up. "How do you reckon the kids are faring?"

"Just fine. But I would not call them kids in front of our son. He believes he is a man, and he will not accept being called anything less."

"In many ways he is a man," Nate admitted, "but in just as many ways he isn't."

"Give him time." Winona wet her mouth, swishing the water with her tongue, then swallowed. "At his age he thinks he knows all there is to know. Only much later will he learn that half the things he thought were true are not and half the things he thought were false are true."

"And one day he'll get to be long in the tooth like us," Nate joked, "and realize he's dumber than a stump."

Winona grinned. "Speak for yourself, husband." Capping the skin, she replaced it. Her legs were in need of stretching, so she slid down and began to walk in small circles. "Do you intend to ride straight through?"

"I've thought about it," Nate said. "But that stretch of trail below the crest is too risky to chance in the dark."

Winona knew it well. For half a mile they would have to wind among craggy heights along a path no wider than her husband's shoulders. A single misstep would plunge them hundreds of feet, to be smashed to pieces at the base. "So we camp just below the rim and start down in the morning?"

"That would put us at the Ward place by late afternoon," Nate said. "I think I know how we can get there earlier—say about noon."

"I am listening."

"Remember that elk trail? The one that forks off below the rim?"

119

"It is longer than the trail down the cliffs."

"Yes, but it's also safer, so we could make better time at night. Once below the timberline, it makes a beeline through some foothills to the stream that flows past the Ward cabin. We could push on until close to dawn, make a cold camp for a few hours to give the horses a breather, and be at Simon's by midday."

Winona liked the idea and said so.

Nate embraced her. The feel of her body against his reminded him of how long it had been since they shared a moment alone. At home Evelyn or Zach and now Louisa were always around. Privacy and parenthood did not go hand in hand. "Too bad we're in such a hurry," he commented.

A grin as impish as Evelyn's spread across Winona's face. "On the way back we will not be."

"I reckon I'll take you up on that, lady." Nate kissed her, reveling in her warmth, her hunger, in how she excited him so tremendously, just as she always did. He had to tear his mouth from hers. "We'd best light a shuck before I get frisky."

Winona recollected the last time he had been "frisky," and her grin widened. "I look forward to our return."

They forked leather and continued on, climbing, steadily climbing, until at long last they entered the pass. Towering walls of solid rock reared on either side. Shrieking wind buffeted them, whipping Winona's long hair and threatening to rip Nate's beaver hat from his head. The temperature had dropped fifteen degrees from what it had been in their valley.

Once through, they found themselves on a wide shelf. A succession of forested slopes unfurled below in sweeping grandeur, like rolling waves in a sea. A tiny dot in the center of the valley was the Ward cabin.

Nate checked for tracks. The most recent were those made by Hap and Vin Coyfield a week before. No one had been through since, which was reassuring. He need not worry about Zach and the girls being stalked while he was gone.

The elk trail was an arrow's flight lower down. Shadows were lengthening as Nate kneed the stallion into it. Within an hour it was so dark he couldn't see Winona's features when he glanced back.

The lower they went, the easier the ride. Nate started to doze off a few times and had to shake himself to stay awake. One of those times, it was a sound that snapped him awake. They were crossing an open bench when from much lower down wafted an eerie shriek. It sounded human, yet not human. Nate couldn't identify the source. Painters were known to scream, but this had been different.

"Did you hear that?" Winona asked. To her it sounded like the screech of a woman in the heat of battle. Shoshone women were sometimes called on to help defend their villages, and would shriek and whoop as lustily as the men.

"I doubt it was either of the Wards," Nate said.

"I pray they are safe, my husband."

"You and me both. As safe as Zach and the girls."

The mountain man was unaware his statement wasn't true. For at that very moment, Jess and Bo Coyfield were camped on the shelf on the south side of the pass. They were sore from their long hours spent in the saddle. Jess was also relieved to be alive. "I don't know about you, Cousin, but that last stretch gave me a few scares."

Bo nodded while adding dry branches to their small fire, built well back from the edge so it couldn't be seen by hostiles. "When those rocks went rattlin' out from under my mule, I thought I was a goner."

A gust of chill wind blew dust down on them from above. "I'll be glad to reach the next valley," Jess said. "Cold never did sit well with me."

"Better get used to it," Bo replied. "My pa says winters

here are fierce. Your breath freezes right in front of your face.''

Jess couldn't conceive of such a thing. "Shucks, he was probably pullin' your leg. It never gets that cold.''

"I don't know. Your ma was in New York once in the winter, remember? She said her snot froze in her nose. Folks there had to go around with their faces wrapped in scarves and such. Here it's likely worse.''

"Do you think we did the right thing leavin' the States? Comin' so far?''

"Where else would we settle? The kin of those people we kilt in Arkansas were huntin' for us. Sooner or later they would've tracked us down and there would've been hell to pay.'' Bo held his hands close to the flames to warm them. "We had to go somewhere they'd never think to look. Somewhere we could start over.''

"I just wish there were more womenfolk hereabouts.''

"Pickin's are slim," Bo agreed. "Cole is takin' that Yankee, and Vin's already staked a claim to Cindy Lou.''

"What's that leave the rest of us? Mary Beth? Unless we start wearin' dresses and grow some new body parts, she wouldn't show any interest.'' Jess sighed. "I guess we'll have to settle for the girls at the King place. Hap will likely want the white one. So one of us will get stuck with the little breed.''

"Don't forget King's squaw. Maybe Hap will take her instead. He likes his women older.''

Jess brightened. "It would be great if he did. Then you and me can flip a coin to see which one of us gets the white girl and which one gets the mixed-blood brat.''

"You can have the white one.''

"Really? How come you're being so generous all of a sudden?''

Bo sank onto his haunches. "I ain't turned Injun lover, if that's what you're thinkin'.''

"Then why?"

"A while back Pa told me Injun gals can please a man in ways a white woman usually won't. Injuns ain't so fussy about their lovemakin'." Bo shrugged. "I'd like to try one, is all. See for myself."

"You'll have to wait a spell. Ma says she's too young yet. What'll you do in the meantime?"

"Promise you won't tell?"

"Tell what?"

"Swear to me, Jess, by all that's holy."

"All right. I swear."

"That's not enough. Swear by the ghosts of our grandparents. And vow to burn in hellfire until kingdom come if you ever breathe so much as one word."

Not another living soul was anywhere within earshot, but Jess moved closer and lowered his voice to vow as his cousin demanded, adding when he was done, "This must be some powerful secret. What, have you been triflin' with one of the mules?"

"No." Bo folded his arms on his knees. "I've been pokin' Mary Beth."

"You're joshin'. She doesn't even like menfolk."

"That she don't. But she lets me take a poke now and again in return for me doing her chores. So I reckon I can hold out until the 'breed is old enough."

"Mary Beth!" Jess said in amazement. "Who would have thought it? I'd of been afraid to even bring it up for fear she'd scratch my eyes out."

"She talks tough. But once you get to know her, she's as harmless as a little kitten."

Simon Ward didn't recognize his attacker until she was almost on top of him. The glint of streaking steel gave him an instant's forewarning as a knife sheared at his throat, and he brought up the Kentucky to parry it. The blade was deflected by the barrel. For a moment they were face-to-face, and Simon saw who it was. "Mary Beth!"

Samuel's daughter snarled and came at him again. Her features were contorted in a feral mask. All semblance of humanity had drained away. She was more beast than woman, a ghoul draped in flesh and blood. Maniacally, she slashed at his arms, at his chest.

Simon rapidly backpedaled, countering her every move. His natural impulse was to shoot or club her. But she was a *woman,* and never once in Simon's whole life had he ever harmed a female. It went against everything his mother and father ever taught him, against all the principles ingrained in him while growing up.

As he retreated before Mary Beth's berserk fury, it occurred to Simon that this was a special case. She was trying to kill him. Surely, given the circumstances, an exception could be made. She even obliged by halting and lowering the knife. He bunched his shoulders to swing, then hesitated, thinking that if he hit her too hard he might kill her.

His hesitation was costly. For in that instant Mary Beth tore into him anew, the knife flashing down low, at his groin. Caught unprepared, Simon nearly lost his manhood. As it was, he skipped backward, barely evading the knife's edge, and then stumbled as his right foot came down on an incline instead of flat ground. Too late, he realized he had blundered. He had stepped *off* the ridge, over the edge. He attempted to dig in his heels to stay upright. Then Mary Beth sprang, slashing as she leaped. The Kentucky warded off her knife but couldn't deflect *her.* She slammed into him.

Simon lost his footing. In a jumbled whirl of limbs they tumbled down together. The earth and stars changed places repeatedly. A hard object gouged Simon in the ribs, and he briefly feared it had been her knife. But whatever it was had been blunt and did not dig deep. A lurching impact separated them. Mary Beth went one way, Simon went another. Desperately, he clawed at the ground with his free hand for support that wasn't there.

Simon had no idea how far the slope went, or how steep it was. He threw his arms to both sides, clutching at thin air. Another jolt sent the Kentucky flying. To safeguard the pistols he placed his hands over them. Seconds later he felt himself bounce, twice, and was pitched into a stand of vegetation. Branches tore at him like daggers as he crashed through thick brush.

Simon began to slow down, which he took as a good sign. He raised his head to see what lay ahead and in so doing exposed it to a large bulky shape in his path. A boulder, judging by the waves of pain that washed over him when he smashed into it. He slid another ten feet, then stopped.

The stars were overhead as they were supposed to be. But they were spinning around and around. And when Simon put his arms at his sides and pushed upward to rise, all of them suddenly blinked out.

Simon Ward dreamed. He was strolling along Third Street in Boston when he felt something poke him in the ribs. Looking down, he discovered that a rock had struck him. Another hit him, and another. Mocking laughter gave the culprits away, a pack of rowdy boys no older than ten or twelve. "Take that!" one of them yelled as they gleefully pelted him. Simon shook a fist. "Savages!" he railed. "Miscreants!" He charged them, only to be hit above the right eye. Blood flowed, and as it seeped over his eyelid, he blinked.

Suddenly Simon was back in the world of the living. Few stars sprinkled the sky. A golden halo to the east explained why. He tried to rise, grimacing when what felt like another rock struck his rib cage. Only, it wasn't a rock. It was the muzzle of the Kentucky.

"About time you came around. I've been jabbin' you for half an hour. On your feet, polecat."

Simon stabbed a hand for a pistol, but both were gone. He slowly sat up, his body so bruised and sore, he felt as if he had been the victim of a buffalo stampede. Mary Beth wasn't much better off. Her right cheek was split, dry blood caked her chin, and her left shin was scraped raw. "What did I ever do to you to deserve this?" Simon asked. "To any of your family?"

"Not another peep. Just stand up and get to walkin'. It's a long ways back."

Arguing with a cocked gun was pointless. Simon rose, his legs protesting. When he applied his whole weight, his right ankle flared with anguish and almost gave way. Carefully, he tested it.

"What's wrong?" Mary Beth demanded. In addition to the rifle, she had both pistols tucked under an arm.

"I think I sprained my ankle when I fell."

"Ain't that a shame." She motioned. "So you'll limp the whole way. It'll slow us down some, but you shouldn't complain. The longer we take, the longer you live."

Simon noticed that the ammo pouch had ripped open and all the ammo spilled out. She had only one shot apiece in each of the guns. Maybe he could use that to his advantage, although exactly how remained to be seen.

"I'm not waitin' forever," Mary Beth said. "You'll limp even worse if I shoot you in the ankle."

Turning, Simon headed for the distant stream. It turned out he had tumbled into a stand of aspens a good sixty yards below the rim. The slope was dotted with large boulders, any one of which could have crushed his skull like an eggshell.

Mary Beth was limping, too, favoring her left leg. "You're the luckiest cuss this side of creation, mister. I wanted to kill you real bad last night for what you did to Tinder. He ain't much as brothers go, but he's always treated me decent." She winced. "I couldn't find you, though, until the sun came up."

126

"Why do you hate me so much? Just because I'm a Yankee?"

"That's partly it. The other part is you're a man."

"So?"

"So men are pigs. There ain't one worth the powder it would take to put a slug in his brain."

"But you just said you're fond of your brother."

"Fond like I'd be for a pet, for a toad or a goat." Mary Beth prodded his spine with the long gun. "Now, quit your jawin'. Tarnation. You flap your gums more than most ten people. How your wife puts up with it, I'll never know."

Simon had over a mile in which to somehow gain the upper hand. Short of rushing her and being shot, he had to rely on his wits. She had calmed down considerably, and since she hadn't killed him when he was helpless, he doubted she would now unless he stupidly provoked her. "As you pointed out, I might be dead before the day is done. Can you blame me for wanting to talk while I still can?"

"Just don't talk to *me*. Jabberin' gets on my nerves."

"Like men do?"

"No, menfolk are worse."

The slope leveled off. Simon could go faster if he were were so inclined. But with his life at stake, to say nothing of the life of the woman he loved, he wasn't about to hurry. Only an idiot hastened to his own execution. "I bet I know why you feel about men like you do."

"Spare me."

"It's because of your family, because of how your father and brothers and cousins behave. But you can't judge every man by the standard they've set. We're not all like they are."

"And how would that be?"

Simon was grasping at the proverbial straw. He knew very little about the clan. They had overpowered him and staked him out so soon after they arrived, he had only random comments and the impressions they had given him to base his comments on. "Take your father, for instance. Always telling you what to do."

"I don't like anyone bossing me around," Mary Beth confessed.

"But in your family you don't have any choice. Whatever your father says goes. I saw how he lords it over your brothers. He must do the same with you. So naturally you've grown to resent it. And because you resent him, you resent all men."

"Go on. This is mighty interestin'."

"No two people are alike. Your father rules your family with an iron fist, but not all fathers do the same. Many fathers are kind and loving. They don't treat their children like slaves."

"Imagine that."

"Their daughters grow up to be normal, decent people. They don't see men as the brutes you do."

"Normal, huh?"

Simon believed he was making headway. "Haven't you ever wished you had a different father? Or different brothers and cousins? They're all the same because they grew up the same. To them, women are cattle to be used as they see fit."

"What's this leadin' up to?"

Halting, Simon faced her. "Just this. Buck them for once. Do the right thing. Help me save my wife and I give you my word I won't harm any of them. All I want is to get her out of there safe and sound."

Mary Beth seemed as if she were pondering the proposal.

"There doesn't have to be any bloodshed. You can sneak Felicity out of the cabin. I'll have two horses ready, and we'll be gone before anyone misses us." Simon smiled when she nodded in apparent agreement. "Your parents will be worried we'll come back with an army of trappers and Indians, so they'll leave. But you don't have to go. You can hide, then come out after they're gone. My wife and I will help you start a new life, free from their shackles. What do you say?''

''I say,'' Mary Beth said softly, leaning toward him, ''that you are the sorriest excuse for a man I ever did see, and that takes some doing.'' She swung the Kentucky's barrel outward.

Simon was unprepared. Pinpoints of light exploded before his eyes, and he tottered as if drunk.

''Did you really think I would fall for that nonsense, mister? I love my kin. They love me. I'd never betray them. Not for you. Not for your sow of a wife. Not for anyone else.''

Her taunts, combined with the pain, pushed Simon's self-control to the brink. Shaking his head, he cleared his vison and saw Mary Beth with her head back, laughing merrily at his stupidity. He thought of how she had been playing with him all along. He thought of the ordeal his wife was suffering. Of his hurt wrists and the wound in his side and his splitting head. Then he did what most any other man would have done.

He snapped.

Uttering a bellow of raw rage, Simon hurled himself at Mary Beth. His right hand wrapped around the barrel and he shoved, but even as he did, her finger closed on the trigger in sheer reflex.

The rifle went off.

Chapter Ten

Felicity Ward hardly slept a wink all night. How could she, with all that was going on?

The Coyfields stayed up until almost dawn, nursing the jug and indulging themselves in other ways. They were as rowdy as drunkards in a tavern, always yelling and laughing. Some of their antics were disgraceful, yet they did them right there in front of Felicity as if it were the most natural thing to do.

The festivities started with a card game. Every member of the clan took part, even the women. Cindy Lou had found Felicity's jar of coins, which Mabel divided evenly among them. The stakes were never more than a few cents, but the Coyfields carried on as if they were wagering hundreds of dollars. They constantly squabbled: over the hands dealt them, over someone trying to peek at their cards, over alleged cheating. It got so that at one point Cole stood up with a hand on a pistol and accused Samuel of dealing from the bottom of the deck. Mabel soothed Cole's ruffled feathers and the game went on, everyone acting as if nothing had happened.

Felicity couldn't understand them. She just couldn't. They were so unlike any family she'd ever met. It bewildered her how they were continually at each other's throats, yet they stood by one another through thick and thin. How they would threaten to do each other violence, how they fired insults back and forth like bullets, yet it was like so much water off a duck's back.

In the end it was the Coyfields against the rest of the world. No matter what any of them did, they'd never turn their backs on one of their own. Such loyalty was admirable, but little else about them was.

After the cards they played dice. They shouted, pushed, howled, and cackled, ignoring Felicity, which suited her fine. She sat in the rocking chair by the fire, knitting so she would have something to keep her hands occupied. Every now and then she caught Cole staring at her with unmistakable lust and she prayed he wouldn't try anything before the night was done.

By one A.M. or so the dice game was over and the Coyfields sat around swapping tall tales and jokes. Felicity was put to work making more coffee. She told them there wasn't much left, that at the rate they were going they would eat her out of hearth and home in a couple of days.

Mabel chuckled and said, ''Don't worry none, dearie. My menfolk are good hunters. As for the other stuff, well, we'll go find some of those pilgrims bound for the Oregon country. Persuade them to part with their victuals.''

At that, most of the Coyfields laughed and snickered.

Felicity did not need to ask them to elaborate. The clan would pick a solitary wagon, swoop down on their unsuspecting victims like a pack of starving wolves, and wipe out every last person. Then they would bury the bodies and bring the wagon back to the cabin. No one would ever guess what happened to the pilgrims, not with all the other dangers travelers fell prey to. The deaths would be blamed on Indians or wild beasts. A hideous yet brilliant plan.

While Felicity was at the stove, Tinder and Cindy Lou ambled to the bed. Right there in front of everyone they fondled one another. Felicity tried not to look or listen, but how could she not? No one else paid any attention. Even when Cindy Lou hiked her dress and slid a hand down Tinder's pants. Even when Tinder pushed Cindy Lou onto her back and took her like a bull elk in rut. Their cries practically shook the timbers, but none of the older Coyfields so much as batted an eye.

Mabel noticed Felicity's flushed features and grinned. "What's the matter, missy? Are you one of those who like to do it in the dark so the husband can't see you?" Mabel picked up the dice for her roll. "Well, that ain't our way. Better get used to the notion, 'cause when your time comes, Cole is just as likely to take you on the floor or on this table as on the bed."

"Have you no shame?"

Mabel reflected a moment. "No, I reckon I don't. We were taught that everything a body does is natural and normal. That we shouldn't feel guilty if'n we like to drink and gamble or whatnot."

"That isn't what I meant and you know it."

Mabel flicked a thumb toward the bed. "You mean that? Hell, sex is the most natural thing of all. Men and women been doing it since Adam and Eve. Where's the shame in lettin' our urges take over?"

"It makes you no better than animals."

"We *are* animals. What else would we be?"

"We're human beings. We're children of God. As different from animals as night from day. We have souls, we have minds. We're meant to better ourselves, not to wallow in the same filth as the hogs."

Mabel arched an eyebrow. "What makes us so special? Haven't you ever read Genesis? How the Almighty put the first man and first woman in a garden with all the *other* animals? About how they were happy there until one day they were filled with that shame you think is so wonderful. Shame because they were naked, as the Good Lord meant them to be. So the Lord threw them out of the garden and

132

they had to fend for themselves.'' Mabel shook the dice. "Seems to me you've got it all backwards.''

No, you do, Felicity almost said. But she held her tongue. Nothing she could say would change their outlook. No argument could make them give up beliefs that had governed their lives for generations.

Soon Tinder and Cindy Lou were done. They slid off the bed, adjusted their clothes, and casually rejoined the rest as if coming back from a Sunday stroll.

Felicity had opened a cupboard and was reaching for the sugar tin when strong arms encircled her waist and foul breath laced with the odor of whiskey enveloped her like a cloud.

"What say you and me go do what they just done?'' Cole Coyfield whispered in her ear.

The insult was more than Felicity could bear. Twisting, she slapped him with all her might. But it was a flea slapping a grizzly, for all he did was smirk lecherously and hold her closer.

"Come on. You'll like it.''

"Never! I would rather die than let you degrade me!'' Felicity drew back her hand to hit him again, but he suddenly grabbed her wrist.

Cole glowered. "You're too damn uppity, woman. I say it's about time someone taught you respect.'' He started to pull her by the arm toward the bed. "I want you, and I aim to have you.''

Felicity held on to the counter and braced her legs. She tried to break loose, but he was immensely powerful. His fingers were like corded iron. She dug her nails in, thinking that would do the trick.

"Keep it up. I like it rough.''

Frantic, Felicity remembered the knife she had used to skin the rabbit. It was still on the counter. Lunging, she grasped the hilt and raised her arm on high. "Let go of me, you vile brute!"

"Do as she says, son," Mabel interjected.

"I want her, Ma." Cole's eyes were pools of carnal hunger. He showed no fear of the poised blade.

"I know, boy. But after you're done she's liable to curl up into a ball and spend days whinin' and sulkin' like some of the others. Granted, a few more pokes and she'll come around, but that'll take a while."

"So why can't I start now?"

"Because we need her in case Nate King shows up. Remember?" Mabel held the jug out to him. "Here. What's left is yours. Then go splash some cold water on your face. Or in your britches if need be."

Cole was loath to obey. Reluctantly, he let go of Felicity, accepted the jug, and downed what remained in one gulp. "For you, Ma. Just for you I'll do it. But it don't sit well with me." He tossed the jug onto the counter, then stormed outside, leaving the door open.

Seconds later Cindy Lou skipped out, too.

Mabel, Jacob, and Samuel were staring at Felicity as if she were the scum of the earth. "You need to be taken down a peg or two, dearie," the mother said sternly. "Now you've gone and got my son all upset. I hate to deny him anything, but it had to be done."

"What was that about Nate King?"

"You're our ace in the hole in case he pays a visit."

Felicity lowered her arm but did not put down the knife. "I'll never help you. With Simon free, you have no hold over me."

"Reckon so, do you?" asked Jacob. "Here I thought the Kings were your friends."

"They are. So?"

Jacob folded his hands on his big belly. "So your husband told us King is due here soon. Might even be on his way already. Whether he lives or dies depends on how well you do what we tell you.''

Mabel remarked, ''We told Bo and Jess to keep their eyes peeled and hide if'n they saw him.''

''What is it you want of me?'' Felicity asked.

''You'll find out soon enough,'' Jacob said, and laughed coldly. So did Mabel and Samuel.

Felicity didn't like the sound of that.

The blast of the Kentucky was deafening. The rifle discharged almost in Simon Ward's face. He wasn't hit, but the flash and smoke so blinded him, he couldn't see Mary Beth. Holding on to the barrel, he yanked, seeking to pull her toward him. The Kentucky jerked forward, the stock dipping toward the ground, and he realized she had released it. No doubt so she could use the pistols.

Holding the barrel with both hands, Simon swung at the spot where she had been standing when she fired. The rifle cleaved the smoke like a sword through paper. She cried out, and he swung again.

This time the Kentucky swished through empty air. Either Mary Beth had ducked or moved. Simon sprang through the gun smoke and there she was, a pistol in each hand, doubled over in pain, an arm pressed to her side where the stock had connected. Mary Beth saw him and uncoiled, bringing the flintlocks into play.

Simon rammed the rifle at her face. She yelped again as it split her cheek. One of the pistols banged, the slug ricocheting off a rock at Simon's feet. That left the last pistol. One last shot.

Mary Beth extended it, taking aim. Simon had no time to swing, so he threw the Kentucky at her. The rifle hit her forearm. She didn't drop either pistol, but she did stumble backward. He was on her before she could recover. Seizing her wrist, he tried to pry the unused flintlock from her fingers. Mary Beth howled and slammed the empty pistol against his temple.

To Simon, the slope seem to dance and swirl. He clung on, standing with his shoulder against hers so she couldn't strike his head again. At the same time he forced her arm backward so she couldn't shoot him.

"Let go of me, you bastard!"

Mary Beth was incensed, her face a vivid hue of red, her eyes blazing with near-maniacal rage. Just as she had been the night before. She was in the grip of a killing frenzy, and the longer he resisted, the worse she became. Screeching like a wildcat, she suddenly sank her teeth into his left arm. It was excruciating. He tugged but she bit deeper, slicing into his flesh and drawing blood.

Pivoting, Simon drove an elbow against her jaw. The blow had no effect, so he levered his arm to do it again. Abruptly, a knee drove up into his groin. Despite himself, his legs nearly gave way.

Mary Beth rammed the knee at him again, but Simon managed to shift and absorb the brunt on his thigh. She surprised him by dropping the spent gun, but it was only to free her hand so she could claw at his face, at his eyes.

Grappling, they teetered back and forth, neither able to gain a clear advantage. Simon couldn't make her drop the second pistol and she couldn't make him stop trying. Mary Beth snarled and hissed, raking his cheek, his chin, his throat. She nearly took an eye.

Their struggle brought them to a rough tract of ground littered with small boulders. Simon was bending Mary Beth's thumb back when she tripped, taking him down with her. Her arm smashed against one of the boulders. The flintlock fell from fingers suddenly numb. Simon grabbed for it, but she screamed pure hate and lashed upward with both legs. Her feet struck him in the chest, knocking him back.

It was Simon's turn to trip. Instantly, he scrambled to his

knees, afraid she had scooped up the pistol and would shoot him. Instead, she held the long knife she kept hidden somewhere under her dress, and now she came at him like a Viking berserker. He had to fling himself backward to keep from having his throat slit from ear to ear.

"You're going to die!" Mary Bath growled.

Simon crabbed backward to put distance between them. There was no reasoning with her now. She was too far gone. Either she would slay him or she would die trying. His hand closed on a fist-size rock, which he hurled as she bounded forward. It clipped her on the forehead, slowing her, allowing him to heave upright.

Mary Beth held the knife close to her waist, the tip angled upward. "I'm fixin' to gut you, Yankee!"

Simon cast about him for something he could use to defend himself. Another rock caught his eye, but as he skipped toward it, Mary Beth lunged toward him. He had to concentrate on her to the exclusion of all else. Again and again she slashed, at his stomach, his face, his groin. Each time he barely avoided the glittering steel.

A crafty look came over Mary Beth and she stopped swinging wildly. Crouching, she circled, seeking an opening, her knife snaking back and forth. Twice she feinted, laughing.

Simon was tiring fast. The past twenty-four hours had taken a fearsome toll. He was exhausted, he was starving. His wrists were in torment, his side throbbed. His head felt as if a mule had stomped on it. And as if all that were not enough, his sprained ankle refused to bear much weight. Eventually, he would become too weak to resist. Mary Beth would easily finish him off. He knew it, and she knew it. Which was why she was toying with him—to wear him out that much sooner.

Simon had to do something while he still had the energy. His desperate plight called for a desperate gamble. To that end, he braced himself, and the next time she feinted, he was ready. Simon flicked a hand out and grasped her wrist. Immediately, Mary Beth hauled backward while simultaneously kicking at his knee. Holding on, he plowed into her.

Mary Beth attempted to spring aside, but Simon's weight bore them both to the ground. She fought like a panther, using her teeth, her nails, her knees. He pressed her knife arm flat, but she heaved against him, almost bucking him off.

"You son of a bitch!"

Simon was counting on his greater weight to keep Mary Beth pinned. But trying to hold on to her was like trying to hold on to an enraged bobcat. She shoved him onto his side, then slid on top, her nails seeking his throat. Simon kept on rolling, carrying her with him, never once slackening his grip. They rolled onto a short slope and careened down it in a tangle of arms and legs.

A tree brought them to a stop, the jolt driving them apart. Simon's ribs were on fire as he rose onto his hands and knees. A broken branch lay a few yards away. Simon dived, swept it up, and turned to confront Mary Beth. Woman or not, he couldn't hold back any longer. He had to end it one way or another.

To Simon's surprise, Mary Beth had not risen. She looked up at him, the fiery glaze gone from her eyes. "Never thought it would end like this."

Suspicious of a ruse, Simon sidestepped to the right to get in front of her. He stopped dead when he saw the hilt of the knife jutting from her chest. A scarlet stain was spreading across her dress. "I wish it hadn't come to this," Simon said. "I'm truly sorry."

Mary Beth pumped onto her knees, swayed, and steadied herself. "Damn my bones if'n I don't believe you." She laughed, then coughed, red drops oozing from the corner of her mouth. "Just my luck to be killed by someone as dumb as a shovel."

"Is there anything I can do?"

"Sure. Pull this pigsticker out and cut your throat with it."

Simon was astonished she could be so flippant with her end so near. "Shouldn't you make your peace with your Maker?"

Mary Beth was staring at the knife. Her eyelids fluttered, she inhaled deeply, and her shoulders sagged. When next she spoke, it was scarcely above a whisper. "Why should I? What did my Maker ever do for me?"

"Gave you life—" Simon began.

"Some life!" Mary Beth said bitterly. "He didn't do me no favors. Havin' a pa who thought I was a growed woman at ten, and a ma who could never tell the difference between menfolk and womenfolk."

"Sweet Jesus!"

"Is he? Then why'd he let me suffer like I done? Why would he let anyone suffer?"

Simon had no answer.

Mary Beth raised tear-filled eyes to the heavens. "I'm not much account, I know. But I did the best I could." A gasp escaped her. She clutched the hilt, trembled as if cold, and died where she knelt.

"I really am sorry," Simon reiterated softly. He wrenched the knife out and wiped it clean on Mary Beth's dress. Next he gathered as many fallen limbs as were handy and covered her to keep predators away until he could return and see to a proper burial. Then he went in search of the second pistol.

It wasn't over yet.

Not by a long shot.

Lou was filling the water trough inside the corral when a shadow fell across her. She turned, not the least bit alarmed, having heard the cabin door open and close moments earlier. "Come to lend a hand? You're too late. I'm about done."

Zach had his Hawken with him. He had spent the past half an hour making sure all their guns were loaded and primed. "Why don't you take a break? I've got something I'd like to say."

"Oh?" Lou's heart skipped a beat. Could it be he was finally going to propose? She hung the bucket from a post and leaned on a rail. "I'm all ears."

She was much more than that, Zach thought, admiring the healthy glow to her cheeks and the redness of her lips. He could not get over how merely being close to her excited him. How her presence seemed to sharpen his senses. His eyes beheld her with crystal clarity, his nose tingled to her scent, his ears hung on her every word.

For her part, Lou wanted to remember this moment forever. It was perfect. Sparrows were flitting in the brush, a jay hopping from branch to branch. The sky was clear, almost as deep blue as the lake, and as still as her breath as she waited for him to speak.

Zach fidgeted, uneasy. He had decided to come right out with it, but now that the moment of truth was upon him, he fretted she might say no and dash his hopes. Suddenly he remembered something. "Where's Evelyn? Have you seen her anywhere?" He didn't want his sister to eavesdrop.

"She was here a while ago," Lou said. "I think she went off to play. Why?"

"No reason," Zach fibbed. "We just have to keep an eye on her so she doesn't get into mischief."

"She promised your father she would behave."

Zach snorted. "You don't know her like I do. She always tells our parents she'll be good, then she turns around and starts a fight with me just to get me in trouble."

"Surely she wouldn't."

"A fat lot you know about girls," Zach said. Realizing what he had just said, he burst into laughter.

So did Lou. She liked how relaxed he had become around her, how at ease she felt around him. As if they had been meant for each other.

Zach stepped closer and leaned the Hawken against the corral. His palms were damper than usual, his throat much drier. Gripping a rail in case his hands started to shake, he began by saying, "I had a talk with my pa before he left."

"What about?"

"Where to live."

"Oh."

"About how I'd like to have a place of my own someday. I always figured I'd live with the Shoshones. Have my own lodge and two or three warhorses and a Shoshone wife. It was my dream."

"And now?" Lou had the impression he was beating around the bush, but she let him get to the point in his own sweet time. Her mother once told her that men often found it hard to say what was in their hearts, that a woman had to be as patient with them as with children.

"Dreams change, I've learned." Zach looked at her and quaked inside. He wondered what was wrong with him. Why was he so scared to utter four little words? *Will you marry me?* What was so hard about that?

"I never had many dreams, myself," Lou said. "Not about the future. My ma used to say that one day a man would come along and I'd fall so hard, I wouldn't believe I was me. If that makes any sense."

Zach faced her. She had made it plain how she felt. All he had to do was ask. He reached for her hand. "I'd better get this out before my tongue freezes up on me. Louisa May Clark, will you do me the honor of—"

"Zach! Lou! Get up here, quick!"

The cry came from behind and above Zach. He whirled,

and was stupefied to see his sister hunkered on the roof of the cabin, gesturing excitedly. "What in the world are you doing up there? Spying on us?"

Evelyn had been doing no such thing and resented being accused. "Pa told us to keep our eyes skinned, remember? I came up here to keep watch and I just saw something. Hurry! Climb on up!"

Long ago their father had nailed short boards to a pine next to the cabin, in effect making a ladder so he could climb on the roof several times a year to sweep off pinecones and busted limbs or do repairs when needed. Until the last year or so Zach had liked to climb up there a lot himself. Snatching the Hawken, he ran around the corner to the tree.

Lou was a few steps behind, doing her best to smother the disappointment that seared her like a red-hot poker. He had been close, so very close. Another few seconds and her heart's desire would have been fulfilled.

Zach scaled the ladder with the agility of a squirrel. The square roof sloped slightly from front to back so rain would drain off. In the center stood his sister. From there a person could scan the valley from end to end. He joined her. "Well?"

"There," Evelyn said, pointing to the west. "They're gone now, but I saw two riders. I swear."

"Whites or Indians?"

"Too far to tell. But they're heading this way. And it can't be Ma and Pa. They're not due back for another couple of days."

Zach scoured the slopes. He saw no one.

"You believe me, don't you?"

"Yes," Zach responded. Evelyn was a tease and a prankster, but she would never joke about something so serious.

Lou scanned the mountains too. "Who else could it be?"

Zach answered honestly. "I don't rightly know. I have a feeling, though, it spells trouble."

Chapter Eleven

The sun hung at its zenith when Felicity Ward emerged from the cabin, bucket in hand, and headed for the stream. She had gone only a few yards when the door opened again and Cindy Lou stepped out. She was holding a pistol.

"Ma says I'm to tag along, city gal."

It had been a rough morning. What with little sleep, worry about Simon, and her nerves constantly being on edge, Felicity was tired and irritable and unwilling to take any more abuse from the Coyfields. "I can get water by myself, thank you."

"Don't give me any sass. When Ma says to do something, we do it. Now, hurry it up so I can get back in there and finish playin' checkers with Tinder."

Felicity was at a loss to understand the clan's raging passion for games. They could not get enough. First thing that morning, Samuel Coyfield had taken a small board and used a piece of charred wood from the fireplace to draw squares on it. Her coins served as the pieces. Since then, the Coyfields had played match after match, the winner taking on all comers until he or she was defeated. Tinder had just beaten Samuel, Mabel, and Cole, and was halfway through a game with Cindy Lou.

Felicity glumly walked on, sarcastically commenting, "I suppose when your family tires of checkers, they'll start on chess."

Cindy Lou sashayed along as if she were parading before

a room of men. "Would that we could. Ain't none of us ever learnt that one. Do you know how?"

"Yes." Felicity's father had taught her when she was seven. One of her fondest memories was of the first time she beat him.

"Then you can teach us! Ma will be tickled pink. She's always said that games keep a person's mind sharp. Hones our wits, like a whetstone hones a knife."

So that's it, Felicity mused. She would rather walk barefoot across a bed of nails than teach the Coyfields anything, but if Mabel insisted, there was nothing she could do. Reaching the bank, Felicity looked out over the valley. The anxiety that had plagued her all morning was rekindled by the sight of a coyote with a rabbit in its mouth. "Shouldn't you have heard from Mary Beth by now? Aren't any of you worried she has come to harm?"

"Ain't likely, Yankee. My cousin can take care of herself. If anyone is hurtin' long about now, it's that puny feller of yours. What did you ever see in him, anyhow?"

Felicity barely held her resentment in check. "Simon is the most wonderful man alive. He's considerate, tender, loving, all the things a man should be."

"Sounds more like a woman than a man. But city men are all like that, I hear. They fret about what clothes they should wear, do up their hair all fancy-like, and then go to operas and silly stuff like that. Sissified, the whole bunch."

"My husband is just as much a man as Cole or Jacob."

"Oh, please. He's not worth a hill of beans. Why, the lunkhead let us waltz right into your home, didn't he? And all that time we were spyin' on you two, he never caught on until there at the end. Pitiful. Downright pitiful."

Felicity would have loved to bean Cindy Lou with the bucket, grab the pistol, and flee, but she couldn't be sure one of the others wasn't watching from the window. She walked down the incline to the gravel bar and squatted to dip the bucket in. The water was cool, refreshing, reminding her of how long it had been since her last bath.

"Rubbed a nerve, did I?" Cindy Lou tittered. "Don't let it bother you none. Pretty soon, you'll be Cole's. Then you won't give a hoot about that Simon no more."

"Shows how much you know. I'll love him with all my heart and soul until the day I die. He's the only man for me."

"Cole ain't poked you yet. Once he does, you won't ever want any other."

So intense was Felicity's hatred at that moment, her whole body quivered. "You people are revolting."

"What brought that on? I done told you the truth. Why hold it against me?" Cindy Lou idly ran a hand up and down the pistol's smooth barrel. "You city gals. The only thing you use your heads for is to keep your ears apart. I should think you'd be happy to land a catch like Cole."

"I'll never let him have his way with me."

"Don't hardly see how you can stop him. Or why you'd even want to. I swear, Yankees ain't got brains enough to grease a skillet."

Felicity could say the same about the Coyfields, but she didn't. The bucket full, she rose and turned, holding the handle with both hands. Her gaze drifted to the high grass bordering the stream, and her heart leaped when she saw who was peering out at her.

Simon Ward had been on his belly for hours, crawling close to the cabin and then waiting for an opportunity to present itself for him to rescue his wife. This was his chance, he believed. Cindy Lou's back was to him as he slowly began to rise.

Felicity guessed his intent and stepped up the bank, complaining, "This bucket sure is heavy."

Cindy Lou snickered. "That's another thing. Why are city

folks such weaklings? Comes from all that soft livin', I reckon. I'm glad I wasn't born there.''

Simon was eight feet away and closing rapidly. He glanced repeatedly at the cabin in case someone else came out.

Felicity pretended it was hard for her to tote the bucket. Holding it low to the ground, her back bent, she marked Simon's advance while keeping an eye on Cindy Lou. "I don't suppose you'd care to give me a hand with this?"

"With a bucket? Lordy, when I was knee-high to a grass-hopper I could lift that with no problem."

"Could you do this?" Felicity asked, and whipped it up-ward.

The water broke over Cindy Lou's face like a small wave. Sputtering and blinking, she stepped backward. "You miserable witch! What did you do that for?"

So you can't see my husband coming up behind you, Felicity thought, smiling as Simon raised his pistol to hit Cindy Lou over the head. Her smile faded, though, when a hulking figure burst from the cabin.

"Touch her and die!"

Simon rotated, saw Cole Coyfield covering him, and wanted to scream in fury. Impaired by his ankle and his fatigue, he hadn't moved fast enough. He had failed, and his wife would suffer on account of it. Unless—unless he was willing to make the supreme sacrifice to buy her time to reach the high grass and get away. "Run, Felicity!" he shouted, darting between her and Cole.

"No, Simon!" Felicity yelled.

Cole's rifle boomed. Simon felt as if a falling tree slammed into his left shoulder. He was spun completely around and his legs swept out from under him. Crashing onto his back, he resisted a cloud of darkness about to swallow his consciousness. He was vaguely aware of Cindy Lou taking the pistol from him, of Felicity kneeling and cradling his head in her lap. "Why didn't you run?" he feebly asked.

"I couldn't desert you." Sorrow racked Felicity, and she cried openly.

The other Coyfields spilled from the cabin. Mabel strode over and leaned down to examine the wound. "Appears the bone is busted, but he'll live. A while yet, anyhow." She smiled at her oldest. "Nice shootin', son."

"Thanks, Ma. We need him alive yet. That pistol he had is one Mary Beth took. He has to tell us where she is."

Tinder pointed at Cindy Lou and exclaimed, "Ain't you a sight, Cousin! What did you do? Go swimmin' with your clothes on?"

"It was this bitch!" Cindy Lou huffed. Moving nearer, she cocked a leg to kick Felicity. "I'm going to stomp the bejeebers out of her."

Felicity raised her head. She didn't care what they did to her, but she couldn't let them kill Simon. She tensed to leap and try to snatch Cindy Lou's pistol. Suddenly, Samuel Coyfield cried out.

"Wait! Look way off yonder! A couple of people on horseback!"

Nate King had seen the whole thing through his spyglass, but he was too far away to help. Now he watched the Coyfields hustle Simon and Felicity indoors. A heavyset woman and two older men reappeared and huddled to urgently discuss what they were going to do. The youngest two did not come back out. Another Coyfield, the one who shot Simon, was hastily reloading. Nate related everything he saw to his wife.

Winona was a study in distress. "You say you saw Simon move? He is alive?"

"Yes. He was holding Felicity's hand." Nate observed the heavyset woman gesture. A hawkish man went to the south end of the cabin. The bear who had brought Simon down

147

glided into high grass and dipped from sight. "They're laying a trap for us." He told Winona what had taken place.

"What will we do?"

Nate closed the telescope with a snap. "We'll ride right into it. They don't know we've seen them. At this distance, they can't see my spyglass." He slid it into a parfleche, then aligned his Hawken across his thighs and loosened both flintlocks under his belt.

Winona liked the fact that he did not offer to ride in alone. He always treated her as an equal, which was more than she could say about other men she had known. "I will take the one in the grass and the one hiding behind the cabin."

"Maybe you should do the talking and leave them to me. I know exactly where the big one went to ground."

"As you wish, husband." Winona cradled her rifle in her left arm. "But what about the two inside?"

"Odds are, they'll come running out to lend a hand. If they don't, one of us has to get in there as quick as we can."

"Felicity and Simon will be at great risk."

"It can't be helped. Simon might be dying now, for all we know." Nate slapped his legs against the stallion to bring it to a trot.

Winona did likewise with her mare. The stick figures in front of the cabin gradually acquired detail and dimension. She was amazed at how obese they were. Among the Shoshones obesity was rare. Oh, some of the women became quite plump after having three or four babies, and a few of the older warriors grew big bellies once they gave up the warpath, but nothing to compare with the Coyfields.

Winona noticed how the woman stayed close to the door to lure them in, while the man drifted toward the creek. It would put Nate and her between them, and flanked by the man in the grass and the man at the far end of the cabin. Quite clever. She was of a mind to rein up well short of the doorway, but to do so would arouse suspicion. So, smiling broadly, Winona willfully put her foot into the jaws of the trap, as it were. She drew rein near the door.

"Howdy, there," the woman declared, as friendly as could be. "I'm Mabel Coyfield. That there is my husband, Jacob. Who might you be?"

Winona introduced herself and Nate, adding, "We were not aware the Wards had visitors. It is wonderful to meet you. I always enjoy making new acquaintances."

Mabel looked as if she had swallowed a live fish. "Goodness gracious! Where'd you learn to talk like that? I swear, you speak English better than I do."

"I have worked hard to master the white tongue," Winona said. Trying not to be obvious, she glanced in the window. Someone was beside it, listening. It was the young man Nate had mentioned, judging by the telltale silhouette. "Are you friends of the Wards, as well?"

"That we are," Mabel declared, putting her hands on her hips within short reach of her flintlocks. "They were kind enough to put us up when our wagon broke down on the way to the Oregon country. Nicer folks you'd never want to meet."

"That is true," Winona said. Movement at the far corner verified that the other man was watching also. Watching and waiting for the signal to attack. Winona studied Mabel and Jacob, debating which one would give it. "Are they inside?"

"Shucks, no. They went for a walk with our young'uns. But we expect them back anytime. Why don't you climb on down and set a spell? You must be tired after your long ride."

Winona made no move to dismount just yet. "Yes, we have ridden far. How did you guess?"

Mabel's right hand was ever so slowly edging forward. "That little filly, Felicity, mentioned you live in the next valley over."

Jacob Coyfield was moving to his left, as casual as could

149

be, pausing after each step. He nodded at Nate and said in genuine envy, "That's a fine rifle you've got there, friend. Hawken, ain't it?"

"Yes," Nate confirmed. He contrived to align it so the muzzle was pointed at the spot where the man who shot Simon had dropped from sight. "Third one I've owned. Best guns made."

"So folks say," Jacob replied. "I've always wanted to get me one, but they were hard to come by in our neck of the woods."

"Where are you folks from?" Nate inquired.

Both Jacob and Mabel answered. Jacob said, "Arkansas." Mabel said, "Georgia." They glanced at each other and laughed.

"We've lived in both places," Mabel clarified. "Now we're lookin' to put down roots somewhere new. Start over from scratch."

Nate never took his eyes off the grass. Some of the long stems shook even though the wind was calm, a yard to the left of where he had the Hawken trained. He shifted the muzzle accordingly. "How many are in your party?"

"Just us and our son and daughter," Jacob lied.

"You'll meet them any minute now," Mabel threw in.

Inside the cabin, Felicity saw Tinder and Cindy Lou swap devilish grins. Tinder was by the window, a cocked pistol held at shoulder height. Cindy Lou was near the bed, where Simon lay sprawled beside Felicity, their wrists and ankles bound and gags in their mouths. From where Felicity was, she could see Winona King through the door. So could Cindy Lou.

Simon groaned softly. He had passed out as they carted him in, and was deathly pale. Felicity was horrified by the stain on his shirt, afraid he was losing too much blood.

Cindy Lou bent down to hiss, "He'd better hush or I'll quieten him myself."

Felicity took the threat seriously. Cindy Lou was itching for a chance to get even for having water dashed in her face.

Over by the window, Tinder motioned at his cousin and whispered, "Pay attention! It won't be long now. I'll put one in the feller, you put one in the squaw."

Felicity looked at Winona again. *The Coyfields were going to shoot the Kings from ambush!* Winona and Nate did not stand a prayer. Somehow, Felicity must warn them. But what could she do, trussed up as she was, and with a washcloth jammed down her mouth?

Outside, Nate King lifted his right foot from the stirrup and crooked it over his saddle. Now he could jump either way if he had to. As ready as he would ever be, he glanced at Winona and tapped a finger on the Hawken, their prearranged cue for what was to happen next. "I'm awful glad to hear there are only the four of you," he remarked.

"How so, Mr. King?" Mabel asked.

"Shortly before we left to come here, a couple of strangers tried to kill my son."

Mabel's good-natured disposition was only skin deep. "What happened to them?" she demanded gruffly. "Did they get away?"

"I should think you'd be more interested in how my son was doing."

"Oh, surely," Mabel caught herself. "I just meant it would be a shame if those polecats weren't made to pay. Did you catch them?"

"My son is fine." Nate deliberately avoided answering her. He had a plan. With Winona and him outnumbered as badly as they were, they had to rely on their wits to give them an edge. His plan called for getting the Coyfields rattled, so rattled they would make costly mistakes.

"And those two strangers?" Mabel prodded.

"That's a story in itself," Nate said, raising his voice a bit so the man in the grass and the one at the south end of the cabin could hear. "I lit out after them. Took me a while, but I caught up."

When Nate did not go on, Mabel took a step and impatiently said, "You fixin' to tell us or leave us in the dark?"

"You really want to hear it?" Nate innocently rejoined.

"Yes," Mabel said, much more harshly than was called for. "I mean, we've had our own share of run-ins with mangy coyotes, so of course we'd be interested." She nodded at her husband. "Ain't that so, Jacob?"

"Sure is, Ma."

Nate pulled his hat a little lower, then nonchalantly rested his right hand on the Hawken. "If you insist. But there's not much to tell. I caught up with them and made them get off their horses."

Mabel was gnawing on her lower lip. "Who were they?"

"They wouldn't say, at first," Nate said. An eyeball had appeared at the corner of the cabin, watching him balefully. And over in the grass, stems had parted enough to reveal a patch of beard and an eyebrow. The Coyfields were being remarkably careless in their worry over their kin.

"But you got them to talk?"

"I sure did. They told me everything."

In the cabin, Tinder Coyfield whispered to Cindy Lou, "Did you hear that? He's talkin' about Hap and Vin! He knows! The bastard knows!"

"Then why did him and the squaw ride right up like they done?" Cindy Lou shook her head. "Nobody is that stupid."

"He's another damned Yankee, ain't he? None of them have a lick of sense."

* * *

On the bed, Felicity Ward quietly twisted and tucked her knees to her chest. She had a hunch what Nate was up to and she wanted to play a part when the bloodbath commenced. Cindy Lou's backside was a leg's length away.

Outside, Winona King was being ignored. The Coyfields were interested only in what her husband had to say. None of them saw her wrap both hands around her rifle, or shift so she faced the front of the cabin.

Nate had paused again, knowing it would annoy Mabel and Jacob and the hidden listeners. He was counting on them to grow a lot more annoyed before he was done—so annoyed, they would give rein to their anger, to their regret. An angry person was a careless person; the angrier they became, the more careless they would be.

"They told you everything?" Mabel Coyfield repeated.

"I had to prod them a little," Nate said.

"Prod them how?"

"As I recollect, I started by breaking the tall one's nose."

Mabel went as pale as a sheet. "You didn't."

"He was stubborn, I'll give him that. He didn't know when he was well off, so I broke one of his fingers."

Jacob Coyfield was also changing color, but he was turning red. "His nose and a finger, both?"

"You'd think that would be enough for most people. Yet he still gave me a hard time. So I shot him in the leg." Nate could see more of the man at the southwest corner, who had rashly exposed half his body in order to hear better.

"Shot him?" Mabel said, virtually choking on the words.

"Twice. The second time was in the head."

Neither Jacob nor Mabel spoke for a full minute. Rage radiated from them like light from the sun. It was Jacob who regained enough composure to ask, "What about the other one? What did you do to him?"

Nate shrugged and gestured. As his hands lowered, they came back down on the Hawken, right where he needed them to be. "What else? After he gave me the information I wanted, I shot him too."

"You killed both of them?" Jacob declared in disbelief.

"They had it coming. They were scheming to murder my whole family." Nate paused one final time. "But I reckon the two of you already know that, seeing as how their names were Hap and Vin Coyfield."

The fuse had been lit. The explosion occurred a moment later when Jacob let out with a bellow and grabbed for his pistols. Mabel was a shade slower. Simultaneously, the man at the cabin's corner stepped into the open and the bear in the tall grass surged erect and brought a Kentucky up.

Nate fired without raising the Hawken. As he threw himself from the saddle, the man in the grass went down. Nate landed on his shoulder, rolled, and came up with a flintlock in each hand.

Winona had also squeezed off a shot, at a youthful visage that filled the window. The face dissolved in a crimson spray as she left the mare in a diving arc. Not an instant too soon. The man at the corner had fixed a bead on her, his rifle spitting lead and smoke. Winona heard the slug buzz overhead.

Nate pointed one pistol at Jacob, the other at Mabel. Jacob was trying to get a clear shot, but the stallion was between them. Mabel had a gun in her hand but couldn't seem to make up her mind whether she would rather shoot Winona or him. When Mabel pivoted in his direction, Nate cored her brain.

Inside, Cindy Lou had brought up her pistol at the first gunshot, taking aim at Winona King. Before she could fire, Felicity Ward slammed both legs outward. Cindy Lou pitched forward onto her hands and knees, glanced back, and snarled, ''You'll die for that, bitch! Soon as I settle with the Kings.''

Felicity started to wriggle off the bed, frantic to do something—anything—to warn her friends. She happened to be staring at the door when it was flung inward and Winona came hurtling through. Cindy Lou jerked up and extended her pistol, but Winona's was already spouting doom.

The ball ripped through Cindy Lou's chest, the impact flipping her onto her back. Her shocked gaze locked on Felicity, and just like that she died.

In front of the cabin, Nate King had one shot left and two enemies out for his blood. The hawk-faced one at the corner was running toward him, unlimbering a pistol. Jacob was coming around the front of the stallion, which nickered and pranced in agitation.

Nate rolled toward the horse. He was almost under its pounding hoofs when Jacob ran into view. Flat on his back, Nate sent a slug into Jacob Coyfield's cranium. Then, pushing onto his knees, he threw himself at the crumpling form, his hands outstretched to catch Jacob's pistol as it fell.

The hawkish Coyfield was almost on top of him. They both fired at the same split second, and Nate felt a tug on the whangs of his buckskin shirt. His shot caught the last Coyfield under the chin.

In three bounds Nate was in the cabin, almost colliding with Winona, who was on her way out to aid him. They dashed to the bed. Winona took Felicity in her arms and began to remove the gag, while Nate bent over Simon.

''It's all right,'' Winona said gently. ''It's over.''

''Thank you, thank you,'' Felicity said, bursting into tears of gratitude. Her relief was short-lived. Suddenly grasping Winona's arm, she declared, ''Dear God! Zach and Evelyn! Are they with you?''

''No. They're at home. Why?''

''The Coyfields aren't all dead! Two left here earlier! They've gone to help some others wipe out your family!''

Chapter Twelve

Evelyn King never listened to her big brother, even when what he told her to do was in her own best interest. He was her *brother,* after all, and she felt he had no right to boss her around. He, on the other hand, thought it perfectly natural to do so. So they squabbled a lot. To get back at him for being bossy, Evelyn would tease him or play pranks. Which resulted in more squabbles.

On this bright and sunny day, shortly before noon, Evelyn was inside playing with her dolls. Her mother had made the first one she ever owned, of a Shoshone woman complete with a beaded buckskin dress and a small parfleche. An aunt had given her another, a Shoshone warrior complete with a tiny bow and shield. Evelyn liked to play at lodge keeping as if the two were husband and wife.

Then there was the doll Felicity had given her, of a white woman with blond hair. It came with two different outfits. Evelyn was changing one for the other when Zach poked his head in the door.

"We're done hobbling the horses. Now no one can steal them without making a racket."

"That's nice." Evelyn tugged at a small sleeve to slide it off the doll's arm.

"We're going to check the trail west of here for tracks. Stay put and keep the door barred. We won't be gone long."

Evelyn did not like his tone. "I'll do as I please, thank you very much."

"Don't start," Zach said. It never ceased to amaze him how she could be so thickheaded.

"It was yesterday about this time we saw those riders. There's been no other sign of them, but for all we know, they might be Coyfields."

"I have my pistol," Evelyn reminded him. She wanted a rifle, too, but her father had not gotten her one yet. He'd promised they would take a trip to St. Louis just to have one custom-made by the Hawken brothers. "I can take care of myself."

"Against grown men?" Zach snorted. "Who do you think you are? A warrior woman?" He rapped on the bar. "Lower this as soon as we leave. I mean it. It's for your own sake."

"I never knew you cared."

"You can be a pain in the backside sometimes. You know that?"

With that, Zach was gone.

Evelyn stared at the door, a trifle sorry she had been so mean. But she just couldn't help herself. Every time he acted high and mighty, something inside of her resented it. She got up to bar the door, then sat back down again. Who did he think he was, ordering her around? She would bar it when she was good and ready.

Evelyn went on playing. She finished changing the dress, then had the two women dolls go for a pretend stroll. "Did I tell you the news?" she had the white doll say to the Shoshone doll. "No," said the Shoshone doll. "What news?" The white doll leaned toward the Shoshone doll. "I'm going to have a baby. We're hoping it's a boy." The Shoshone doll snickered. "Why would you want a boy? All they do is give everybody a hard time."

Evelyn set down both dolls and stood. She supposed she should do as her brother wanted. She walked to the door, but instead of barring it, she opened it.

All morning Evelyn had been cooped up indoors. She

wanted some fresh air, wanted to stretch her legs. The cries of waterfowl made her think how nice it would be to stroll down to the lake to watch their antics. The ducks were always good for laughs, the way they chased one another and dived and quacked.

Returning to the bed, Evelyn picked up the Shoshone doll and said, "Keep an eye on our home while I'm gone. If anyone comes snooping around, give a holler." She lined up the three dolls side by side, then took her pistol from its peg on the wall and walked outside.

Evelyn squinted in the bright sunlight. It felt wonderful to have the sun on her face and the wind fan her hair. Humming, she skipped on down the path. A robin chirped in a nearby tree. A butterfly flitted by.

Evelyn loved the woods. She loved the animals, the birds and cute bunnies and funny chipmunks and things. Not grizzlies, since they ate people. And not painters, ever since that one tried to eat her. Oh, and not rattlesnakes, since they might bite her. But just about everything else she liked.

The lake was tranquil. Evelyn went to her special spot and sat on a small, flat boulder. The ducks were up to their usual antics. She watched a green-headed one chase a blue-headed one, then marveled at how they could dive and stay under for what seemed like minutes before they came up with small fish in their beaks. She couldn't hold her breath half as long as they could.

In the trees something rustled. Evelyn looked but saw no cause for alarm. It was probably the wind, she reasoned. A tiny voice in her head said it might not be, that she should head for the cabin right away. That she should bar the door and stay there until Zach and Lou got back.

"I'm staying right here," Evelyn said aloud. She would show Zach. She would prove to him she was able to take care of herself.

Evelyn went on watching the ducks and geese. A big old

goose was mad at a red-headed duck and kept chasing it whenever it swam too near. She laughed when the goose nearly pecked it on the head. They were so silly. Almost as funny as chipmunks.

An osprey winged in low over the lake. It must not have seen her, because it flew directly toward where she sat, veering away when it was close to shore. Grinning, Evelyn followed its flight, turning her head as it banked to the north and arched up over the trees. Then her whole body went as cold as ice.

At the base of the trees stood two men. Young men, about her brother's age, only they had scruffy beards and wore scruffy clothes and floppy hats. They were staring at her and smirking.

Evelyn slid off the boulder and gripped her pistol in both hands. *Coyfields!* the tiny voice in her head screamed. Then again, maybe they weren't. Trappers passed through the valley all the time. She took a step back and brought the pistol up, just in case. It would do no good to run. They were only fifteen or twenty feet away and would catch her before she reached the trail.

"Howdy, sprite," one of them said good-naturedly. "We didn't know there was anyone else hereabouts."

The pair came toward her, smiling, friendly.

Evelyn wagged her pistol. "That's close enough. My pa says I have to be careful of strangers."

The skinny one laughed and elbowed his companion. Neither of them stopped.

"I mean it!" Evelyn warned. To show she was serious, she thumbed back the hammer. At the click the two men halted.

"Now, hold on there, girl," said the skinny one. "We don't mean you no harm. Honest. We're just passin' through, is all. Got us a camp up the valley a ways."

The heavier one nodded. "Put the gun down, child."

Evelyn was not about to do any such thing, and said as much. "And I'm not a child. I know how to use this pistol, so don't come any closer. I've shot plenty of things." Which was an out-and-out lie. Evelyn could never bring herself to harm another living creature.

The heavy one scowled, but the skinny one went on smiling and responded, "Ain't no need to put lead in anyone, darlin'. We'll go away if that's what you want. But won't you at least tell us your name?"

Evelyn saw no harm in that, so she did. "Who are you two?"

"I'm Jess," the skinny one said. "This here is my cousin, Bo. We're right pleased to meet you, little princess."

Evelyn did not see how anyone so polite could be much of a threat. She lowered the pistol a trifle. "My brother will be back soon. Stay here until he does and I'll bring him down to meet you."

"Where are your folks?" Bo asked.

About to answer, Evelyn suddenly realized it might not be smart to tell the truth. "Oh, they were here a minute ago. They won't be gone long."

Bo and Jess grinned at each other.

"Nice meeting you." Evelyn began to back off. The two men were not acting as if they intended to harm her, but it wouldn't hurt to run to the cabin and bar the door as Zach had wanted.

"Hold up there, darlin'," Jess said.

"Yeah," Bo declared. "Why are you in such an all-fired hurry to go when you just told us your folks are comin' back any second?"

Evelyn thought fast. "I'm to wait for them inside."

Jess slowly advanced. "Mind if we mosey along? We sure would like to meet your ma and pa. You see, kin of ours are missin'. We're hopin' maybe your folks have seen 'em."

"That's right," Bo said. "His brother and mine. We came

across some Injun sign west of here, so we're a mite worried."

"No Indians have been through our valley in a good long while," Evelyn said, continuing to back away. "Unless you count the Shoshones. But they're more like family."

"None of you heard any shootin' recently?" Jess inquired.

"No." Evelyn did not like how they were slinking forward like a pair of sly foxes stalking a grouse. She steadied the pistol. "That's far enough. Please. I don't want to hurt you."

Both men stopped, but they did not seem very happy. Bo turned to Jess and said, "I just don't get it. If this 'breed is tellin' the truth, what could have happened to Vin and Hap? It ain't like them to up and disappear."

Evelyn recalled hearing those names before. "Vin and Hap!" she blurted. "They're the coyotes who tried to kill my brother! The ones my pa killed! You two must be Coyfields!"

The change that came over them was startling. Their smiles faded like twilight into night, and dark, ugly clouds loomed on their bushy brows. They reminded Evelyn of the ogres in a fairy tale she had read.

"Your pa killed our brothers?" Bo was ablaze with hatred. "Then I reckon it's only fair we repay the favor." He took a step, but Jess grabbed his arm.

"Hold on. Ma wanted this little one and the white girl alive, remember?"

"She doesn't know about Hap and Vin. If'n she did, she'd do just like I'm fixin' to do." And with that, Bo raised his rifle.

Fear rooted Evelyn in place. As much fear as she felt that time the mountain lion tried to eat her. Maybe more. Then she realized Zach and Lou were bound to hear the shot and come running, right into the guns of the Coyfields. She couldn't let that happen. As much of a nuisance as her brother was, he was still her brother, and she loved him. As the muzzle of Bo's rifle centered on her chest, she jerked on the trigger of her pistol.

An invisible fist smashed into Bo's right shoulder, spinning him half around. He tottered and would have fallen if Jess had not caught him. Jess glanced at Evelyn, exclaiming, "I'll be damned! She did it!"

Bo sagged to his knees. "Get her! Gut the half-breed bitch!" He shoved his cousin.

"Don't worry about me! Do it."

Evelyn pivoted and fled for her life.

Zachary King had an ulterior motive for checking for tracks. Other than when hobbling the horses, he had not been alone with Lou since Evelyn spotted the two riders. Most of the time they had stayed indoors, keeping vigilant watch at the window and gun ports. Evelyn had always been close by, and Zach refused to propose with her around. She might laugh or poke fun and spoil the moment.

So Zach had thought up the idea of checking for tracks. He felt it was safe to leave Evelyn alone for a while. Almost twenty-four hours had gone by, and everything was fine. Maybe Evelyn really hadn't seen them. Maybe she only thought she did. Or maybe they had been Indians. Utes, perhaps, hunting for elk. There were any number of possibilities.

Now, winding along the trail their family routinely used to reach the west end of the valley, Zach mustered his courage once more. It didn't help matters that Lou hadn't said much to him since the day before. She was upset, and Zach was at a loss as to why. He worried she was having second thoughts, that when he proposed she would jilt him.

Little did Zach know, it was just the opposite. Louisa was heartbroken that every time he tried to ask her, they were interrupted. She was dying for him to try again. *Please, please, please,* she inwardly begged.

Lou noticed Zach glancing at her as they walked among the stately pines. She grew excited, knowing him well enough to guess he was building up his nerve to ask again. To encourage him, she slipped her hand into his and gently squeezed.

Zach smiled and pecked her on the cheek, his confidence restored. A log beside the trail was as good a spot as any, so he walked to it and sat. A stray beam of sunlight bathed Lou's face as she perched next to him. She was so incredibly lovely, she took his breath away.

Lou wondered why Zach suddenly looked as if he had been hit on the noggin by a club. His eyes had a dazed quality about them. "Are you all right?"

The question puzzled Zach. "Sure. Why wouldn't I be?"

"You look a little strange, is all."

"Strange how?"

"Oh, I don't know. As if you aren't feeling well."

"I've never felt better." Zach was embarrassed. He must be so nervous, it was showing.

"Am I red in the face? Do I have a rash? What?"

Lou was sorry she had brought it up. "No, no. You're fine. Believe me."

"I feel fit enough to wrestle a bear."

"You look *fine*."

Zach hoped so. At an important moment like this, he wanted to be at his best. Which was peculiar, since he had never been one to primp and preen. He wasn't like those who fawned over their own reflection.

Lou decided not to open her mouth again until he was done. She waited, and waited, but he was deep in thought, apparently bothered by what she had said. Men were so odd at times. Just as her mother always claimed.

Zach was breathing deeply and slowly. He had to stay calm. He couldn't make a fool of himself. Propping the Hawken against the log, he took both of Lou's hands in his. "I reckon you know what this is leading up to. I never thought I would say this about any woman, but I love you, Louisa May Clark. I love you with all my heart."

Lou tingled from head to toe. *Finally* her dream would come true! "I love you, Stalking Coyote."

Somehow, a feather or what felt like one had gotten into Zach's throat, and he had to cough before he could go on. "I've already talked to my pa about us having a place of our own. But now I need to know if you want to live with me. Lou, will you make me the gladdest man alive by becoming my—"

To the east a gun cracked.

In a twinkling Zach was on his feet. "That was a pistol shot! Evelyn must be in danger!" Down the trail he flew, with one very perturbed young woman in his wake.

Evelyn scooted up the trail faster than a jackrabbit, but it wasn't fast enough. Jess Coyfield was rapidly gaining and would overtake her well before she reached the cabin. Stopping, she hurled the flintlock at him. As heavy as it was, it took all her strength, but she was rewarded with an oath when it hit his shoulder.

"Damn you, gal! Don't make this harder than it has to be!"

Evelyn darted into the woods. Either he was making some sort of odd joke only adults would understand, or he was the stupidest person alive. Why would she make it easy for him to kill her? She weaved among the trees, seeking to lose him in the undergrowth. A glance revealed he was sighting down his Kentucky. Without delay, Evelyn angled to the right, putting a cluster of pines between them.

Evelyn had spent countless hours playing in that area. Her goal was a cluster of boulders, her favorite hiding place when her brother was on the warpath. She would secret herself until Jess Coyfield gave up searching. Crackling brush told her that he was after her again, closing the gap quickly.

"When I get my hands on you—!" he hollered.

Evelyn was tempted to shout back, "You never will!" But that might have been just what the man wanted. He might have been trying to trick her so he would know where she was. Coming to a wide trunk, Evelyn dashed behind it and stood stock-still. She heard him barreling through brush, then the woods were suddenly quiet.

He was listening, Evelyn guessed. He had lost track of her. So long as she didn't move, she was safe.

That was when a yell pierced the air from the vicinity of the cabin.

"Evelyn! Evelyn! Where are you?"

Cupping her mouth, Evelyn was going to alert her brother about the Coyfields. Movement not ten feet away silenced her. The skinny one was much too close. If she shouted, he would be on her before she could get away.

"Sis! Are you all right! Answer me!"

The worry in her brother's voice surprised Evelyn. She would never have thought he cared so much.

"Evelyn!" This was Louisa. "If you can hear us, please answer!"

Evelyn would like nothing better. But Jess Coyfield hadn't moved. What should she do?

Zach was beside himself. He had rushed into the cabin, found it empty, and burst back out. He'd scoured the ground, but finding the most recent set of her prints in the jumble by the cabin was a feat that would daunt his father. So he had called out, his apprehension mounting when there was no response.

Lou had never seen Zach so shaken up. She half hoped Evelyn was playing a prank, that Evelyn had fired the shot just to rattle them.

Zach gazed toward the lake. His sister was always going

there to watch the ducks or doodle in the dirt. It would be just like her to have gone again after he left, to spite him. He sprinted down the trail at breakneck speed and was half-way there when a figure materialized ahead, where the trail met the shore. A stocky, bearded man in homespun clothes, hunched over, shuffling like a wounded buffalo.

"You there!" Zach shouted.

The stranger snapped erect. A reddish stain on his right shoulder explained why he had been staggering. On spying Zach, he awkwardly jammed a Kentucky rifle to his left shoulder.

Zach tensed to fling himself into high weeds, then remembered Lou was close behind him. *The ball would strike her!* Spinning, he tackled her just as the Kentucky thundered.

Lou did not know what was going on. She did not see the man with the rifle until she was thrown to the ground.

Her elbow cracked hard, numbing her arm. Lou tried to rise, but her arm gave way. The next moment Zach had her about the waist and literally hauled her into the undergrowth. His lips brushed her ear.

"It's another Coyfield! Stay down while I circle around."

On the other side of the trail, Evelyn heard the rifle shot and panicked. *They were shooting at her brother!* She hurtled around the tree, heedless of her own safety, and paid for her folly when a scarecrow appeared out of nowhere and snagged her on the fly.

"Now I've got you!" Jess Coyfield gloated, dangling her by her wrist as if she were a varmint he had caught in a trap.

Evelyn did what came naturally. She threw back her head and screamed at the top of her lungs.

Louisa May Clark had just seen Zach vanish to the east. She never hesitated when Evelyn's cry rang out. Rising, she crossed the trail in a single leap. Off to the right, motion pinpointed where she would find Evelyn. A skinny man was brutally shaking her. Lou's rifle seemed to spring up of its own accord. "Let go of her, damn you!"

Jess Coyfield started, cast Evelyn down, and shifted, his Kentucky rising as his thumb locked on the hammer.

He would have been better off dropping the rifle, too.

Crouched behind a stump, Zach saw the wounded Coyfield hasten up the trail. The man held a pistol now and was moving much more briskly. Zach had heard his sister's scream, but there was nothing he could do, not until he had disposed of this threat. Thrusting his Hawken onto the top of the stump, he aligned the sights with the man's torso.

The crash of a rifle to the south brought the Coyfield to a stop. It took all of Zach's self-control not to spoil his aim by looking up.

"Over here!"

The man whirled. He squeezed off a shot without really aiming.

Zach's aim was dead-on.

It was not quite half an hour later that Nate King galloped up to the cabin in a shower of earthen clods. He was astride a sorrel belonging to Simon Ward and had about ridden the animal into the ground. Before the sorrel stopped moving, he was out of the saddle. Nate took several strides, then saw Evelyn by the cabin door, playing with her dolls. She glanced up and smiled sweetly.

"Hi, Pa."

Nate was too flabbergasted to do more than respond in kind. "Hi," he said, looking right and left for evidence of their enemies. The whole ride back, fresh tracks had spurred him on. Tracks made by Jess and Bo Coyfield. Nate had been certain he would arrive to find three cold bodies.

"You're home sooner than we thought you'd be. Where's Ma?"

"She's staying with the Wards for a while. We're going to join her tomorrow."

Feeling foolish with his cocked Hawken trained on empty air, Nate lowered it. "Simon has been hurt, but he'll recover. He should be back on his feet inside a month."

"That's good to hear. I like him an awful lot."

"Anything happen while I was gone?"

"Not much. Zach was being bossy. One of my dolls is having a baby."

"Anything else?"

"Oh, a couple of men tried to kill us."

"And?"

"We killed them instead."

The tension that had driven Nate to the limits of his endurance melted away like snow under a hot sun. He had gone almost three days with hardly any sleep, and suddenly he was so tired, his legs felt wooden. "Where are your brother and Lou?"

"Down at the lake. I wouldn't bother them, though, if I were you."

"Why not?"

"They told me that if I went down there, they'd shoot me."

"What?" Nate turned to go have a talk with his oldest. But a gleeful shout made it unnecessary. It was the cry of a young woman who was supremely happy, whose fondest wish had just been granted, and who wanted the whole world to know.

"Yes! Yes! A thousand times yes!"

#45
WILDERNESS
IN CRUEL CLUTCHES
David Thompson

Zach King, son of legendary mountain man Nate King, is at home in the harshest terrain of the Rockies. But nothing can prepare him for the perils of civilization. Locked in a deadly game of cat-and-mouse with his sister's kidnapper, Zach wends his way through the streets of New Orleans like the seasoned hunter he is. Yet this is not the wild, and the trappings of society offer his prey only more places to hide. Dodging fists, knives, bullets and even jail, Zach will have to adjust to his new territory quickly—his sister's life depends on it.

Dorchester Publishing Co., Inc.
P.O. Box 6640
_5458-2
Wayne, PA 19087-8640
$5.99 US/$7.99 CAN

ZANE GREY

RANGLE RIVER

No name evokes the excitement and glory of the American West more than Zane Grey. His classic *Riders of the Purple Sage* is perhaps the most beloved novel of the West ever written, and his short fiction has been read and cherished for nearly a century. The stories collected here for the first time in paperback are among his very best. Included in this volume are two short novels and two short stories, plus two firsthand accounts of Grey's own early adventures in the territories that he so notably made his own. Zane Grey was an author who experienced the living West and wrote about it with a clarity and immediacy that touches us to this day.

Dorchester Publishing Co., Inc.
P.O. Box 6640
Wayne, PA 19087-8640

5212-1
$5.99 US/$7.99 CAN

Please add $2.50 for shipping and handling for the first book and $.75 for each additional book. NY and PA residents, add appropriate sales tax. No cash, stamps, or CODs. Canadian orders require $2.00 for shipping and handling and must be paid in U.S. dollars. Prices and availability subject to change. **Payment must accompany all orders.**

Name: _____

Address: _____

City: _____ State: _____ Zip: _____

E-mail: _____

I have enclosed $_____ in payment for the checked book(s).

***CHECK OUT OUR WEBSITE!** www.dorchesterpub.com*
_____ Please send me a free catalog.

RIDERS TO MOON ROCK

ANDREW J. FENADY

Like the stony peak of Moon Rock, Shannon knew what it was to be beaten by the elements yet stand tall and proud despite numerous storms. Shannon never quite fit in with the rest of the world. First raised by Kiowas and then taken in by a wealthy rancher, he found himself rejected by society time after time. Everything he ever wanted was always just out of his grasp, kept away by those who resented his upbringing and feared his ambition. But Shannon is determined to wait out his enemies and take what is rightfully his—no matter what the cost.

PETER DAWSON

FORGOTTEN DESTINY

Over the decades, Peter Dawson has become well known for his classic style and action-packed stories. This volume collects in paperback for the first time three of his most popular novellas—all of which embody the dramatic struggles that made the American frontier unique and its people the stuff of legends. The title story finds Bill Duncan on the way to help his friend Tom Bostwick avoid foreclosure. But along the trail, Bill's shot, robbed and left for dead—with no memory of who he is or where he was going. Only Tom can help him, but a crooked sheriff plans to use Bill as a pawn to get the Bostwick spread for himself. Can Bill remember whose side he's supposed to be on before it's too late?

Dorchester Publishing Co., Inc.
P.O. Box 6640
Wayne, PA 19087-8640

___5548-1
$5.99 US/$7.99 CAN

Please add $2.50 for shipping and handling for the first book and $.75 for each additional book. NY and PA residents, add appropriate sales tax. No cash, stamps, or CODs. Canadian orders require an extra $2.00 for shipping and handling and must be paid in U.S. dollars. Prices and availability subject to change. **Payment must accompany all orders.**

Name: _____

Address: _____

City: _____ State: _____ Zip: _____

E-mail: _____

I have enclosed $_____ in payment for the checked book(s).

CHECK OUT OUR WEBSITE! www.dorchesterpub.com
_____ Please send me a free catalog.

LOREN ZANE GREY

AMBUSH FOR LASSITER

Framed for a murder they didn't commit, Lassiter and his best pal Borling are looking at twenty-five years of hard time in the most notorious prison of the West. In a daring move, they make a break for freedom—only to be double-crossed at the last minute. Lassiter ends up in solitary confinement, but Borling takes a bullet to the back. When at last Lassiter makes it out, there's only one thing on his mind: vengeance.

MAX BRAND®

JOKERS EXTRA WILD

Anyone making a living on the rough frontier took a bit of a gamble, but no Western writer knows how to up the ante like Max Brand. In "Speedy—Deputy," the title character racks up big winnings on the roulette wheel, but that won't help him when he's named deputy sheriff—a job where no one's lasted more than a week. "Satan's Gun Rider" continues the adventures of the infamous Sleeper, whose name belies his ability to bury a knife to the hilt with just a flick of his wrist. And in the title story, a professional gambler inherits a ring that lands him in a world of trouble.

NIGHT OF THE COMANCHEROS
LAURAN PAINE

In these two brilliant novellas, celebrated author Lauran Paine perfectly captures the drama of the frontier and the gritty determination of those who lived there. In "Paid in Blood," an inept Indian agent has put the Apaches on the warpath, and U.S. Army Scout Caleb Doorn is all that stands between the bloodthirsty braves and the white settlers. The title story tells of Buck Baylor, who returns home from his first cattle drive to find his father murdered and the countryside in the unrelenting grip of vicious outlaws. Will Buck be able to avenge his family before he, too, is killed?